DOO TO
DANGER

LUKE TEMPLE

Luke Temple was born on Hàlloween 1988. When he was 10, Luke didn't enjoy reading, he was terrible at spelling and he found writing hard work. Yet today he's an author! When not behind his desk with his writing partners, a one-eyed dog and a bald hamster, Luke spends most of his time visiting schools and bringing his stories to life with the children he meets.

Collect all the 'Ghost Island' series:

☐ Ghost Post

☑ Doorway To Danger

☐ The Ghost Lord Returns

Other books by Luke Temple:

☐ Stormy Cliff

☐ The Secret Theatre

To find out about Luke Temple and his books, including fascinating facts, fun videos, interviews and hidden secrets, visit:

www.luketemple.co.uk

DOORWAY TO DANGER

LUKE TEMPLE

Gull Rock Publications

For Mum and Dad

With thanks to Jessica Chiba, Kieran Burling, Anne Finnis, Gareth Collinson and the 'Temple Team' at Highfield Hall Primary School

www.luketemple.co.uk

Copyright © Luke Temple 2012
Cover and illustrations © Jessica Chiba 2012

First published in Great Britain by Gull Rock Publications

The paper used in the printing of this book has been made from wood grown in managed, sustainable forests.

ISBN: 978-0-9572952-1-6

Printed and bound by CPI Group (UK) Ltd, Croydon, CR0 4YY

A catalogue record of this book is available from the British Library

A short extract from
The Dark Side Of Thistlewick Island
(second edition) by Sandi Foot

Thistlewick Island got its name when adventurer Lord Samuel Lewis Thistlewick discovered it in 1712 and set up his own community here. Thistlewick is a very beautiful place, from the crystal blue waters at its southern tip to the rugged, rocky cliffs at its most northerly point. Don't let that beauty fool you, though – Thistlewick Island also holds many dark secrets.

Lots of these secrets involve the forest, a three kilometre stretch of tall, twisted trees that stands between the main town on south Thistlewick and the farms at the north of the island. Over the years a number of people have wandered into the forest and never returned, and on a small island rumours spread quickly. Some islanders think there are human-eating wolves in the forest, bigger than any man; others think the place is haunted by evil spirits; the shepherd, Walter Carrot, is convinced the trees themselves trap people in their branches.

When Thistlewickians have to pass through the forest, there is a safe path that they never dare stray from, and children are forbidden to play amongst the monstrous trees.

But as all children know, when you are told not to do something, it just makes it all the more tempting…

Thistlewick Island

Explore an interactive map of Thistlewick
at: **www.luketemple.co.uk/map.html**

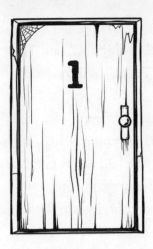

People Are Coming

'There are people coming!' Thatch shouted, floating into the third-floor bedroom as fast as he could manage.

'People!' Peter shrieked.

'Careful, Peter. Don't use up too much energy,' said Willow, placing her hand on his shoulder to calm him.

'Will we have new friends to play with?' Rose asked eagerly. 'Is one of the people a girl?'

'It's a girl and a boy,' said Thatch.

'How old are they? Are they my age?' asked Peter, now bouncing up and down.

'The girl looks about Rose's age, the boy about my age.' Thatch grinned.

Rose spun around in excitement. Peter stopped bouncing and his eyes welled up. No one his age ever came; he was always left out.

'Don't be such a crybaby,' said Thatch.

'Be kind to Peter,' Willow said sternly. 'He's only young.'

Peter had been six years old when he died. Willow still remembered watching it happen, seeing him panic, unable to help – she had never cried so much. That must have been over forty years ago.

Thatch rolled his eyes. 'We're all ghosts, what difference does age make? I've been stuck here much longer than he has.'

Willow looked down at the floor. Suddenly, any excitement about the people coming towards the house disappeared, replaced with a great fear. She had been in the house longer than all the other ghosts – over ninety years. She knew all too well what happened to people who stepped through the front door.

'Are they definitely coming this way?' Willow whispered.

'I saw them out the front.' Thatch hovered eagerly by the door. 'Come on, we need to get moving, or we'll never reach the front door in time to see them come in.'

'Is it safe to move?' asked Willow. '*He* isn't about, is *he*?'

'No, I think *he* is sleeping. We're safe.'

Thatch, Willow, Rose and Peter moved out of the room.

The procession down the stairs was slow. The ghosts

needed energy to move; they mainly got this from the heat around them, but there wasn't much of that about at the moment. The house was almost unbearably dark and cold.

Only Thatch had found a way to conserve energy whilst moving quickly.

When they reached the second-floor landing, Willow held onto Rose and Peter's hands. She never felt safe wandering around the house, and always stayed alert to danger. Thatch sailed through the air ahead of them. Willow knew he enjoyed the risk of moving from room to room.

'Slow down,' she said through gritted teeth. '*He* will notice us.'

'If you want to miss seeing these people arrive, fine,' Thatch replied in his loudest voice. 'Anyway, stop fretting – I haven't seen *him* for ages.'

'I have felt *his* presence around us,' said Willow. Rose nodded. 'And if new people are coming, you know *he* will be desperate to get to them before we do.'

Thatch glared at her and soared down the next flight of stairs.

Willow looked around cautiously. Gripping the two younger ghosts tightly, she calculated the best place to hide if *he* appeared, before travelling towards the front door. Thatch was there, gazing out of a small pane of glass.

'Can you see them?' asked Peter nervously.

'Do they seem playful?' asked Rose.

'Quiet, you two, I'm trying to look,' said Thatch.

The other ghosts glided up to the window and peered out together.

Thatch was right – a boy and a girl. It was too dark to see them properly, but Willow squinted her eyes and stared closely. The boy was tall and thin, with short blond hair that was almost spiky. Willow didn't know much about boys, but this one had a look on his face that reminded her of Thatch in a bad mood. The girl had a mop of hazelnut hair, pushed back from her face, revealing shining eyes that Willow could only describe as adventurous.

'She's wearing trousers!' Rose exclaimed. 'Why is the girl dressed in boy's clothes?'

'Maybe girls do that now,' said Thatch.

Just then, the girl looked towards the house. All the ghosts gasped. Peter backed away. The girl was staring through the glass, directly at them.

'Can … can she see us?' Peter asked breathlessly.

Thatch frowned. 'No, she … she can't… We don't have enough energy to be seen. Not even I do. We're too weak.'

The girl looked back at the boy, standing a couple of metres behind her.

'I thought not,' Thatch said more confidently. 'She

was just staring at the house, not us.'

'Listen. The boy is speaking,' said Rose, pressing her ear to the glass.

'You've got to be joking, Becky,' they heard him say.

The girl grinned at him. 'Come on! You're the one who said we should come this way, Finn.'

Becky and Finn, Willow thought, fear now running through her. *Please do not come any closer. Run away! Do not enter this house!*

Doorway To Danger

'What is this place, anyway?' asked Finn.

'I don't know. Oh, hang on.' Becky pushed aside some overgrown weeds and found a rotting wooden sign. 'It says this is Thicket House.'

'We should get back home.' Finn turned to go. 'It's getting late and I promised my granddad I'd help him at the harbour tonight.'

The two children had been travelling for a long time now. They had met early in the Thistlewick Island market square and headed up to the dark forest at the centre of the island – the place their parents had forbidden them to play, where even adults feared to tread.

There was one safe path through the forest, but Becky and Finn had quickly strayed from this, and soon became lost. Becky hadn't really worried, though – the forest didn't seem that scary, and she knew it would be hard to find what she was looking for. Like finding a piece of hay in a stack full of needles. For hours all they had seen was a maze of trees – big ones, small ones, fat, thin, all contorted into creepy shapes. Then the building had appeared, like a mirage in a desert, drawing them near.

Maybe this is the right place, Becky thought.

She stood staring up at it – Thicket House.

It was surrounded by the most ancient trees Becky had ever come across, no sunlight penetrating their canopy. But even in this gloom, she could see how old the place was. A huge expanse of moss and creeping plants covered the crumbling brickwork. Most of the windows had been boarded up, with thick iron bars covering them, like a prison cell; the rest were grimy and cracked. On the roof there were one and a half chimneys; the other half lay on the path in front of the two children. Thicket House looked like it should have fallen down years ago.

Becky's eyes lit up. 'Come on, let's go inside.'

Finn groaned. 'What? Seriously?'

'Why not? You said the forest is your favourite part of Thistlewick and you're not scared like everyone else.'

'Yeah, well, I've never been to this part before,' he mumbled. 'I didn't even know there was a house in the forest.'

'So you are scared.'

'No!' Finn replied fiercely. 'It's just… You haven't even said why you wanted to come into the forest. What are you looking for?'

'You'll find out soon. Now, let's have a snoop around Thicket House!'

Becky walked up to the low front door in the dark porch. Before she even put her hand on it, the door started to creak open – like it was inviting her in. She took a deep breath of thick forest air and crossed over the threshold.

The hallway seemed just as old as the outside of the house, but it wasn't so run-down. Everything was undisturbed and in its place – a coat rack, a table with a candle on, a painting under a tall staircase. All covered in a thick layer of dust.

Becky's mind filled with questions, each one a rope pulling her further into Thicket House. How long had it been like this for? Who would build a house so deep in the forest? Did anyone still live here?

As she moved forwards, Becky felt something cold brush past her. The door slammed shut.

'Careful, Finn,' she said.

'It just closed by itself,' he replied.

'Well don't make such a racket.' Becky turned back to face the hallway. 'Hello? Is anyone here?' Her call echoed strongly around the building.

No reply.

'Hello?' she tried again.

'Leave my house,' came a low whisper from somewhere nearby. 'Or I will get very angry.'

Becky gasped. 'Who is that? Why do you want me to leave?'

Silence. But Becky felt something large brush against her back.

'Did you feel that, Finn … Finn?'

She turned around and jumped backwards in shock, a dark shadow looming towards her.

Then she realised what it was.

'Don't be an idiot, Finn.' She pulled off the coat he had wrapped around himself and hit him with it. 'This isn't the time for your stupid pranks.'

Finn laughed. 'You fell for it, though.'

'I wish Jimmy had come, not you.'

'What, your stupid science geek of a best friend? He wouldn't come into the forest – he'd run away screaming like a girl.'

Becky shot a furious glare at Finn and moved through a doorway to the right.

Jimmy had abandoned her to go on holiday. But while he was in Switzerland visiting the Large Hadron Collider, Becky had discovered something in a notebook – something that had made her desperate to go searching in the forest. The notebook had also said that she should take someone with her, and Finn had seemed up for an adventure. Becky had forgotten how annoying he could be – she should just have come on her own!

The room she entered was lined on one side with a large collection of books; there were three moth-eaten armchairs and a long rug. In the wall opposite her was a large stone fireplace and above that a mirror.

'Whoever did live here must have used that fireplace a lot. It's freezing, isn't it?' said Becky.

Finn wandered in and shrugged.

'Let's make a start,' she said. 'Bring the bag over here.'

They sat down on the rug and Finn handed Becky a large bag. Out of it, she took a small glass bottle and four candlesticks and candles. She placed the bottle on the floor and the candles evenly around it.

'What exactly are you going to do with a bottle and four candles?' asked Finn.

'Use them to catch a ghost.'

'Oh no.' Finn rolled his eyes. 'I knew this was going to be about ghosts! Ever since you found that ghost in the post office, you've been obsessed with them. And now you've dragged me all this way so you can try to catch another one.'

'I'm a ghost hunter, Finn. That's what I do. And this isn't any old ghost. This is the ghost of Eric Pockle.'

She struck a match and held it against each of the candles. One-by-one the flames came to life. In the darkness of the room, they cast four powerful beams of light.

'We're ready to begin,' said Becky.

Bottling

The four ghosts gathered around the candles.

Willow felt breathless. 'They're trying to find Eric! That's who they're searching for. It must be the same one, Thatch – the same Eric that came to this house?'

Thatch glared at her. 'Don't mention that man!'

'Eric was nice, Thatch,' Rose piped up. 'Why are you always so mean about him?'

'Nice? Ha! Shows what you know.'

The ghosts paused their argument to listen to Becky addressing the room in general. She asked if Eric was there, and whether he would like to use the energy from the candles.

'Heat! Energy! She wants us to take her energy!' Peter exclaimed.

'Poor Peter,' said Willow. 'You have been starved of energy for years. We all have.'

Rose looked up at her. 'Can we take the energy from the candles?'

'I don't know,' Willow replied truthfully. 'Let's just wait a—'

But Peter was gliding towards the candles, transfixed by their brightness, their warmth. He stopped by one of them and gave a small shiver of excitement as its heat passed through him. Then he moved into the centre of the candles, right over the bottle, so he could get heat from all of the candles at once.

Suddenly he was full of energy! He started spinning around, jumping in the air.

'I got energy! I got energy!'

'I wouldn't do that if I was you,' said Thatch.

Peter stopped dancing. 'Don't spoil my fun! Every time I do something, you stop me. It's not fair!'

'Yeah, Thatch, stop spoiling his fun!' Rose joined in.

'Fine, if you want to get bottled, carry on,' said Thatch, screwing his nose up. 'Why don't you join him in there, Rose? You can both be bottled for all I care.'

'What does that mean? Getting bottled?' asked Willow.

'Eric knew all about bottling,' said Thatch. 'That man who you all think was so nice tried to bottle me. It nearly worked as well, but I managed to escape before he put a cork in the bottle. Otherwise I would have spent the rest of time stuck in there!' said Thatch.

'What happens? How does bottling work?' asked Rose.

'If a ghost hovers over the bottle, in the middle of the candles – like Peter is now – when they have taken the energy from all the candles, they get sucked into the bottle. And just imagine, all your particles crushed into that tiny space.' Thatch grinned, looking directly at Peter now. 'All jumbled up, your feet particles by your ear particles, your eye particles by your bum!'

Rose let out a gasp.

'I was only stuck in Eric's bottle for a few seconds, but they were the worst seconds I've ever had. I was so confused I just wanted to scream. It was worse than dying!'

The candles around Peter started to flicker ominously. He shot quickly away from them and into Willow's arms.

'That wasn't very nice, Thatch!' she said.

'Yeah, well bottling's not nice, and that's what these children are trying to do to us.'

Willow looked down to Becky and Finn. He was kneeling there looking deeply annoyed, she was sitting up straight, eagerly waiting for something to happen. They didn't look like they meant any harm. Those poor children.

'Do you hate Eric because he tried to bottle you, then, Thatch?' asked Rose.

'Not just because of that,' said Thatch. 'He also broke his promise to us, remember.'

'He did not!' said Willow. 'I know he didn't.'

'Yeah right.' Thatch rolled his eyes. 'Anyway, I'm going to take their energy. Look, Peter, this is how you're meant to do it.'

Thatch positioned himself safely on the outside of one of the candles. He rubbed his back against the flame and stuck his tongue out at Peter.

The small ghost burst into tears and fled into the corner of the room. Rose followed him.

'Don't cry, Peter,' she said. 'Don't waste all your new energy on crying.'

The flame that Thatch was taking energy from suddenly went icy blue. In a second, it went out.

Becky gasped. 'Look at this, Finn.'

'One of the candles blew out, so what,' Finn replied.

'It went *blue*! The flame only goes blue if there's a ghost near it.'

Thatch had moved over to the next flame and was busy sucking the energy out of it.

'Was that you, Eric?' Becky asked. 'Was that the ghost of Eric Pockle?'

Thatch chuckled. The second candle flashed blue and went out. He moved onto the third and extinguished it almost instantly.

Becky was looking excited, saying, 'One candle to go, Eric. Keep going!'

The final flame flickered madly and went out.

Willow's eyes lit up. 'Thatch. You could use the energy you've just taken to reveal yourself to Becky.'

'Why?' asked Thatch. 'You know how much energy it takes to appear in a form that living people can see. That would wipe all my new energy out completely!'

'But if you reveal yourself, you can tell Becky what we know about Eric.'

'No way, I'm not wasting energy doing that.'

'Be careful then, Thatch,' said Willow. 'It's dangerous carrying that much energy around. *He* is near, I can feel *him*. *He* will take it from you. Rose, Peter, come on, I am taking you back upstairs, before *he* appears.'

Thatch gave them a menacing grin. 'You run away, then. I'm going to have some fun!'

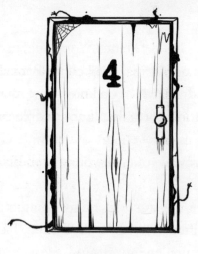

Run!

When the final flame blew out, the room was plunged into darkness once again.

'So what now?' asked Finn. 'Did you catch him?'

'No,' said Becky, staring closely at the bottle. 'It didn't work. I'm sure there was a ghost there, though. It could have been Eric.'

She started to pack the candles away.

'Who is this Eric person, anyway? Why do you want to find hi—' Finn's head whipped around. 'Did you hear that?'

'What?'

'That!'

Becky stared at him. 'I told you, don't be an idiot.'

Finn walked over to a window and stared out. 'There's nothing here. For a minute I thought…'

Thud!

The noise sounded like it had come from above them. Like something had hit the ceiling.

'Finn, stop fooling about. I know it's just you playing another practical jo—'

Becky's head jolted forward as something hit the back of it. It couldn't have been Finn – he wasn't close enough. She turned around to see at least ten books pulling themselves out of a shelf and flying straight towards her.

'Duck!'

The two children threw themselves behind armchairs. A huge puff of dust rose up as the books collapsed to the floor.

Becky peeked over the back of her armchair to see if it was safe to move. In front of her, one book was still floating. It was open to page 18, with the heading 'Chapter 4: Run!'. The book slammed shut, sending a load of dust straight at Becky. She couldn't help breathing it in. As she coughed and spluttered, trying to clear her throat, she heard a noise. It was coming from under Finn's armchair.

Tap, tap, tap-tap. Tap, tap, tap-tap.

Finn slowly bent down and peered under the armchair.

Tap, tap, tap—

'Aaaahhhhh!'

Finn shot backwards. From under the chair came a

long, pointed fire poker. It hovered menacingly in front of him. He edged away, but the poker followed.

Finn made a run for it – to the opposite corner of the room. The poker fired itself towards him like an arrow.

'Finn, move!' Becky shouted.

Just as it looked like the poker was going to hit him, Finn dodged sideways. Becky ran for the door. Finn caught up with her, but so did the poker. It charged towards them at an ever-increasing speed. They fell out of the room and Finn just had time to shut the door behind him. He collapsed against the door, breathing deeply.

Thwack!

Finn turned his head slowly to the left. There, standing out from the wood, barely centimetres from his left ear, was the sharp point of the poker. It had embedded itself in the door.

'Did a ghost throw that at me?' he asked.

Becky nodded, her heartbeat racing, her mind excited. 'I think … that whoever we tried to bottle … they're a bit angry.'

'Then we need to get out of here,' said Finn.

He went over to the front door and tried turning the handle.

'It's really stiff!'

He pulled as hard as he could, but it wouldn't budge.

Tap-tap. Tap-tap.

The noise came from the floor above them. Becky looked up the staircase, intrigued. Was that the same ghost, or was there more than one in the house?

It was the final straw for Finn.

'That thing's going to attack me again. Why isn't the door opening?!' he shouted. 'It must be locked. Maybe we can break out through that boarded-up window.'

Tap-tap. Tap-tap.

Finn grabbed hold of a plank of thick wood nailed to the window on the right of the front door and tugged.

Tap-tap. Tap-tap.

'No good, it's firmly stuck,' said Finn. Panic stretched across his face as he looked around the hallway. 'We're trapped!'

The Ghost Hunter

The children waited silently to hear where the tapping noise would come from next.

But after a minute there had been no other sound.

'Whatever that was, it seems to have given up, for now,' said Becky.

Finn didn't say anything, and when Becky looked at him, a darkness – a shadow – seemed to be stretched across his face. He staggered forwards a bit. The shadow moved away from him, leaving his face very pale.

'Are you OK, Finn? You don't look well.'

'We need … to … get … out…' He flumped down at the bottom of the staircase. 'It feels like … like all my energy's … been sucked out of me.'

'That's weird. You were fine a minute ago.' As she spoke, Becky felt strange too. Her eyes blacked out

23

briefly, as if she was about to faint, and she collapsed down beside Finn.

'Did you bring any food?' he asked. 'It feels like I haven't eaten all day.'

Becky nodded. 'There's some in the bag.'

Finn searched through the contents of the bag. 'Blimey, you've got a lot of things in here.'

He pulled out blankets, electric fans, jumpers and a torch before he found the food.

'Why so much stuff? It's like you were planning to go camping or something.'

'A ghost hunter needs to be prepared for everything that might happen. That's what it says in my notebook.'

'I bet you weren't prepared for getting stuck in this creepy place, though.'

The two children tucked into a cheese sandwich gladly – half of it each.

'What is this notebook you keep going on about?' asked Finn.

Becky pulled a small, creased black book out of her pocket and showed it to him. 'Mayor Merryweather gave it to me recently. It used to belong to Eric Pockle. He was Thistlewick's ghost hunter.'

'Before you came along…' Finn commented.

'This notebook is where Eric recorded all his ghost hunts. Have a look at the back.'

Finn took the book and, with a shaky hand, flicked

to the last page. At the top it read 'Ghosts Seen On Thistlewick'. Under this was a list of names.

'What am I looking for?'

'The bottom name.'

Finn found it and frowned. 'Eric Pockle? Why is Eric written in his own notebook as a ghost seen on Thistlewick?'

'That's what I wondered,' said Becky. 'I went to see the mayor to ask what happened to Eric. He said that the last time Eric was seen, he was going on a big investigation in the forest. There have always been rumours about the forest, haven't there?'

'Sure,' Finn agreed. 'People think everything from werewolves to witches and wizards live in it, Granddad says.'

'Well, Eric had heard a rumour about something evil and ghostly in the forest and went to find it.'

'What happened to him?' asked Finn.

Becky shrugged and finished her half of the sandwich, still feeling quite weak. 'Mayor Merryweather doesn't know. No one does. All that was ever found of Eric was his notebook.'

'If Eric's name is written at the back of the notebook, then he must have died and become a ghost, because someone saw his ghost and wrote his name here.'

'Exactly,' said Becky. 'That's why we've come into the forest, Finn. Now I'm Thistlewick's new ghost hunter,

I want to see if I can find Eric's ghost and ask what happened to him.'

'So have we found him? Was that Eric's ghost chasing us?'

'I don't think so. Eric sounded like a nice person from what Mayor Merryweather said – quite shy and quiet. A ghost has the same personality as the person they came from, and I don't think a nice ghost would throw a fire poker.'

'Then, if Eric isn't here, what about the evil ghost he was looking for?' asked Finn. 'You don't think that's what threw the fire poker, and locked us in here?'

'It was definitely an angry ghost of some kind.' Becky felt a bit stronger now. She looked at Finn, who didn't seem as pale, then stared up at the ceiling. 'The last time we heard the tapping sound it was coming from up there, wasn't it?'

'You're not going to try and find it, are you?'

Becky grinned. She reached into her bag and took out a box the shape of a calculator.

'What's that?' asked Finn.

'An electromagnetic field detector.' Reading the puzzled expression on his face, she explained, 'It helps me find ghosts. Electromagnetic fields are all around us, but ghosts are meant to give off loads of electromagnetism. I can use this to check around the house – if the detector gives a high reading, we'll know there's a ghost about.

Look.' She pressed a button on the detector. 'It says zero point five, which means—'

Becky was cut off by a sound very much like a snorting pig. She looked up to see Finn with his head hung down, snoring. That proved he was feeling better – he was being annoying again. She stood up and debated whether to hit him or not. She settled on stamping on his foot.

'Ow! What was that for?'

'You might find what I'm doing boring, Finn, but it's important! If there is an evil ghost in this house, then I have to find out more about it. If you're so bothered about getting out of here, why don't you stay out of my way and try to find a key for the front door or something?'

She turned round and stomped up the stairs, kicking dust back towards him.

'Fine!' he called after her. 'But if I find the key, I might just escape and lock you in again.'

***

Becky took a general reading of the upstairs landing. A number flashed up on the EMF detector's screen: 0.7.

'No ghosts up here,' she said. Any reading below 1 was normal. Only a number over 2 would make her suspect a supernatural presence.

There were four doors leading off the landing. One by one, she opened them carefully, aware that if she did find a ghost, it might be the angry one that chased them. The first three doors led to rooms you would expect to find in any old house – an ornate bathroom, a large bedroom with a four-poster bed and a smaller room that looked like a study. The windows in all the rooms were boarded up, making them just as dark as downstairs. As she scanned the EMF detector around, each room had a normal reading.

The fourth door gave Becky a bit of a surprise. There wasn't a room behind it, but a staircase leading to a third floor.

'Odd,' she said.

She waved the detector up the stairs. A number came up on the screen – 0.5 – normal. She was about to move away, when the number slowly started to rise. It passed 1 and 2, eventually stopping at 2.7.

'There's something up there.'

Becky tentatively placed a foot on the first stair.

Crack!

She pulled her foot away quickly. In the wood she had trodden on a thick crack appeared. She looked cautiously up the staircase and saw that the wood was rotten and there were cracks and gaps all the way up it. The staircase wasn't safe to climb. If there was a ghost up there, it would just have to stay there.

Becky closed the door and walked back towards the stairs leading down to the hall. The temperature changed around her. It had already been freezing, but Becky's face suddenly felt like it had turned to ice. The landing was darker too, like a large shadow had swept over it.

She started to feel faint again and her legs were wobbly. It was like Finn had said earlier – the energy had been sucked out of them.

Bleep, bleep.

It was the EMF detector – Becky hadn't realised it could make a sound. She looked down through blurry eyes and saw numbers flashing madly across the screen – from 0 to 10 and back again. This was too much for the device to cope with. It gave a final *bleep*, then the word 'Error' appeared on the screen.

An uneasy feeling crept over Becky as the landing got darker still. Mustering up her strength, she ran down the stairs, and crashed into Finn in the hallway.

'You look like you've seen a ghost,' he said.

Becky caught her breath. 'I think there might be two ghosts up there, and one of them must be really powerful. It just broke my EMF detector, and that's never happened before.'

'It's the evil ghost Eric was trying to find, isn't it?' The panicked look appeared on Finn's face again.

'I'm not sure. But Eric's notebook says that when it comes to ghosts, powerful usually means dangerous,' said Becky. 'I think you're right, Finn, we should get out of here. Have you found a key?'

'There's a problem with that idea,' Finn replied. 'Go and look at the front door.'

Becky walked over to it. At first, she couldn't see what he meant. Then she looked at where the keyhole should be.

'There isn't one. There's no space for a key. How has the door been locked if there's no key?'

'Exactly,' said Finn.

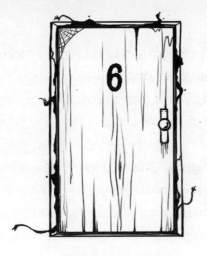

No Way Out

'Help! Help!' Finn called out.

'Why are you doing that?' asked Becky.

'Join in. Someone might hear us.'

'In the middle of the forest, where barely anyone dares to go? There'll be no people within a mile of this place.'

'It's worth a try,' said Finn.

Becky looked to the left of the hallway and saw a door they hadn't been through yet. 'I'm going to see if there's a way out through there. You can stay here and ask all the trees for help, if you want.'

She left him calling out and went over to the door. It creaked open. She wasn't entirely sure what the room she stepped into had been used for – it was small with six sides. Becky thought for a minute what a six-sided shape was called; maths was one of her least favourite subjects at school.

'Hexagonal,' she remembered. 'This room's hexagonal.'

Other than its odd shape, the room was much the same as the others. The window was boarded up and cobwebs stretched over the ceiling. The only object in the room was a large vase, which was similar to one that Becky's mum kept her granddad's ashes in at home.

This made Becky think about Eric and how he had died in the forest. Maybe it *was* his ghost the EMF detector had found at the top of the cracked stairs behind the door. But then she remembered the weakness she had felt, and the way the EMF detector had broken. What if Finn's fears were true and an evil ghost was also inside Thicket House?

Come on, Becky, she told herself. *You can find a way out.*

In one of the six sides of the room was a second door. Through this Becky found a kitchen – long and thin with cupboards running along either side, and a very old-looking stove to the right. She walked the length of the kitchen and behind the next door came upon some stone steps, which led to a cellar. This contained a rubbish bin, a few rotting boxes and a fireplace. The cellar had no windows – of course it didn't, Becky realised, because she must be under the ground now.

So why was there a metal door at the other end of the

cellar? In all the houses Becky had been in before, the cellar had just been a big storeroom, with only one way in and out. Maybe the metal door led to more stairs, or a secret tunnel – a way out of the house!

She tried opening it. The door was heavily rusted, but eventually she forced it open and a wall of cold air hit her. She shivered and moved forwards – into a tunnel!

For a moment she really did think she had found a hidden exit as she felt her way along the tunnel. But it quickly ended and came out into another room. Her eyes had to adjust even more to the darkness here – while the other rooms in the house had the faintest of light in them, this one seemed pitch-black. It was also freezing cold.

Eventually she began to see the silhouetted outline of the roof of the room, which was a circular domed shape. The floor of the room was piled high with. something familiar. Becky bent down and felt it – straw.

'Why is there an underground room full of straw?' she wondered.

However odd it was, the room definitely wasn't a way out of the house and Becky had hit a dead end. She stepped out of the room and shut the door.

As she did, she sensed something moving behind her and turned, expecting to see Finn standing there. But he wasn't. On the wall opposite her a shadow started forming – but there was nothing there to cast one. Becky jumped back. Her left arm started to shake, but not just out of fear. Her left leg joined in, then her right. She fell to the floor, her energy stripped away. Her head started to spin and her vision darkened.

She tried to focus her eyes on the cellar steps and crawled over to them. Becky gripped hold of the bottom step and pulled herself upright. Using the wall as support, she scrambled up the steps.

Only when she got back to the hexagonal room did Becky begin to feel her normal self again.

'There's definitely something weird going on here.'

The sooner she and Finn got out of Thicket House the better.

She walked back into the hallway. Finn was nowhere to be seen.

Becky noticed that the door with the fire poker stuck in it was slightly ajar. Had he dared to go back in there?

She peered around the door. 'Finn?'

A groan came from the floor.

'Finn? Finn! What have you done? Are you OK?'

He was lying in a heap by the fireplace, covered in thick black soot.

'I tried climbing the chimney,' he said slowly. 'Got so close to the top, but banged my head and…'

Finn moved his hand downwards, demonstrating how he had fallen. He was looking even paler than he had before – something had drained all the energy out of him too.

Becky went back into the hall and grabbed her bag. She took a blanket out and wrapped it round him.

'Can you get up, Finn?'

'I think so … I haven't broken anything … I just feel so weak.'

Becky helped him over to one of the armchairs, which he slumped into gladly.

'The chimney's too small at the top to fit through,' said Finn, in barely a whisper, 'so we can't escape that way.'

'There's no way to get out from the other side of the house, either, or upstairs,' said Becky.

Finn tried to say something, but it was now a great effort even to open his mouth.

Becky looked around the room. She knew she had to find a way out of the house. But if an evil ghost was lurking around the place, she should stay near Finn until he was stronger. She thought about what she could do, then took a small pot of salt out of her bag. She began scattering the salt in a circle around the armchairs.

Finn whispered something that sounded like, 'What you doing?'

'In his notebook, Eric says you can use salt to keep evil ghosts away.' Becky took the notebook out of her pocket, flicked to the right page and read, '"Salt is pure and natural, whereas evil spirits have unnatural, negative energy. That means they can't cross over a line of salt.

People pour salt across their doorways to stop evil ghosts getting in." So maybe if I pour a circle of salt around us, that will stop anything evil in this house from harming us.' She poured the last of the salt out of the pot and completed the circle. 'I really don't know if it will work.'

A snoring sound came from Finn again. But this time he wasn't bored and pretending – he was genuinely asleep.

Becky curled up in a blanket in the chair next to Finn. She stayed awake for a long time, watching over him and worrying about how they could get out. Eventually, though, her weakened body gave in, her eyelids grew heavy and she drifted off to sleep, hoping that nothing would harm them.

The Shadow

A man stood in front of Thicket House, a large bag slung over his shoulder. He was quite old, but, even in the gloom of the forest, his eyes were bright and his thick glasses twitched on his nose with excitement.

He went in…

The man charged around the downstairs rooms, trying to find a way out. The front door wouldn't open, there was no keyhole in it, and the windows were boarded up. He was trapped!

'How could I be so stupid?!' the man exclaimed…

He investigated each room carefully, calling out, asking if ghosts were there. In one room he set up a bottle and some candles. He nearly captured something, but it didn't work…

Dark shadows passed in front of him and he felt very weak. He knew now that an evil spirit was here. He rubbed herbs into the cracks in walls, poured salt across doorways, but it didn't do much good...

The man sat in an armchair in the room with all the books. Cold and pale, he bit into some mouldy bread. He must have been here for days now. The man had lost track of time. Every night he woke from a terrifying nightmare. Every day he exhausted himself trying to escape. The brightness in his eyes had faded. It was so, so cold. And now he was eating the last of his food...

The man continued exploring the house, searching every room, every nook and cranny. He wouldn't give up! With no energy left, it took him such a long time, spending hours in each room. He didn't know what he was looking for now. And every so often a fear would take him over, a terrible panic from somewhere unknown...

He awoke with a start, and found himself standing, swaying at the top of the staircase. All the energy had been sucked out of him. He had nothing left to fight with. Something pushed him and he fell. He reached the bottom of the stairs with a crash and collapsed into a corner. As the man looked up a shadow swept towards him. He shielded his eyes with a hand, as if the shadow

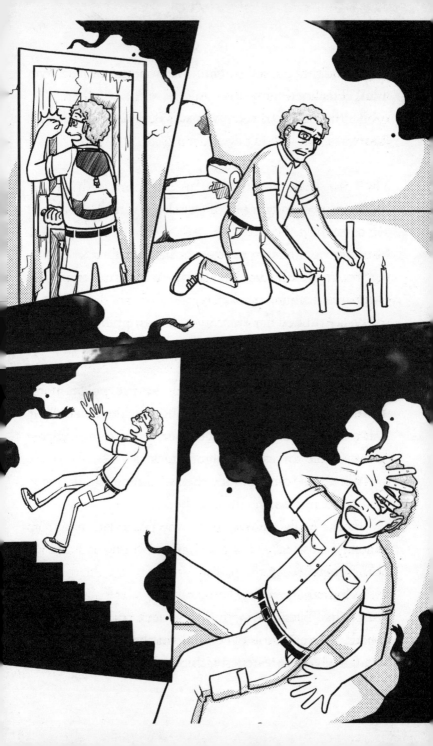

was a bright, blinding light. The shadow moved over him, consumed him.

All that could be seen now was darkness.

***

Becky bolted upright out of her sleep. What had she just seen?

Finn was standing nearby, staring at her.

'You were shaking,' he said. 'A lot. And shouting. Were you having a nightmare?'

Becky rubbed her eyes. Sweat was dripping down her, but she felt freezing. 'I suppose I was.'

'I had a nightmare too.'

Becky noticed that Finn had the fire poker in his hand. He'd obviously braved going outside the circle of salt and removed it from the door, ready to use against any invisible forces that might attack.

'What was yours about?' she asked him, wondering if he had seen the same thing as her.

'It was really strange. I saw my granddad, but from when he was really young – nearly as young as I am. He was somewhere in the forest.'

'What was he doing?'

'He had been playing hide-and-seek with his brother, Thatch. Even though Granddad had forbidden it, Thatch always threatened to hide in the forest. So when

Granddad couldn't find his brother, he thought he must have gone into the forest. I saw Granddad going around shouting, "Thatch? Where are you?" It carried on for a whole hour – just Granddad wandering, getting more and more worried.'

'Did he find Thatch?'

'No. Thatch went missing, a bit like Eric did. What was your nightmare about?'

'I think I actually saw Eric, trapped in this house,' Becky replied, and went on to explain exactly what had happened. 'Are you sure they were nightmares, or did we have visions?'

'What do you mean?' asked Finn.

'Ghosts can give you visions, replaying events from the past – it happened to me with the post office ghost.'

'I think it was just our imaginations working overtime,' said Finn. 'Granddad has told me a bit about Thatch before – that he went missing and was never found, but he didn't say where Thatch went missing. I guess that was just my mind playing tricks on me, remembering your story about Eric dying in the forest.'

'But my nightmare seemed so real. It could have been Eric showing me visions about what happened to him.'

Finn looked at her doubtfully. 'You still think Eric's in this house?'

'I don't know. How are you feeling now?'

'I can move about, but I'm still not great. It's freezing

in here.' Finn looked to the fireplace. 'Do you think we could light a fire?'

Becky looked around the room – there was no way of telling if it was safe to move outside the circle of salt. But she was chilled to the bone too.

'Let's give it a go,' she said.

The house may have been dark and cold, but it wasn't damp. That meant the wood in the basket next to the fireplace was still dry and good to use. Finn placed some of it in the grate, while Becky fetched some matches from her bag. She struck one and placed the flame against the wood. Soon a roaring fire was going, making the room look golden and giving it more light than it had probably seen for years.

It was a wonderful feeling as Becky started to warm up. Finn came over and held his hands up to the fire. But as quickly as it had started, the fire went out.

'Odd,' said Finn.

'Did you see what colour the flames were when they went out?' said Becky.

'Oh, they were bright blue. Does that mean it was a ghost?'

'Yes.'

'Eric?'

'No, a normal human ghost couldn't do that,' Becky said, her heart starting to beat faster as she realised: 'It must be the ghost that broke my EMF detector.'

'The dangerous one?'

Becky nodded. Her eyes darted around the room. Then a shadow came from nowhere – like it had in the cellar. It crept over her and her vision suddenly went.

'Becky? Becky, are you OK?' Finn sounded concerned. 'You're shaking. Becky, stop it.'

But Becky couldn't. She was so weak that it felt like she was a prisoner, locked up and dying of starvation.

'I … I don't…'

She crumpled onto the floor. The shadow left her and she regained her senses. Looking up, she gasped as she saw it forming again – this time over Finn. His eyes closed, he swayed backwards and forwards, then he collapsed down next to her.

Becky dragged him along the floor away from the fireplace and back into the circle of salt. Fortunately, the salt seemed to be protecting them, because the shadow didn't follow. Instead, it slowly disappeared.

Becky was sure now that the shadow wasn't just an ordinary shadow. It was the shadow that was sucking their energy away – maybe it was the shadow that broke her EMF detector too. And she was certain that it was the same shadow that had chased Eric in her nightmare.

The shadow, therefore, must be the evil ghost Eric had been searching for.

Willow's Risk

After taking Rose and Peter back to the safety of the third-floor bedroom, Willow had returned to keep an eye on Becky and Finn. She had watched through worried eyes as Thatch's antics with the fire poker woke *him* up. *He* has been furious and chased Thatch away, then focussed *his* attention on Becky and Finn. *His* prey.

He had started by trapping them in the house, which was how it always began. The same thing had happened to Willow, all those years before. She remembered it so well. Then, when she was a ghost, she had watched it happening to Thatch, Peter and Rose – and Eric, of course. After that, *he* slowly and painfully fed off their energy, until they were too weak to even try to escape. Then death came.

He had started the process with Becky and Finn

already – Willow had seen them getting weaker in their efforts to escape from the house.

After *he* had taken their fire and disappeared, Willow slipped out from the bookcase she had been hiding behind and watched as Becky and Finn fell back to sleep.

She smiled at the fire poker Finn still held – ready to attack, even in his sleep. With her bright blue eyes closed to the world, Becky looked troubled. Willow wanted desperately to tell her about Eric. Why did it have to take so much energy to reveal yourself to living people?

The ghost girl would never take the children's energy like *he* did. But she had to talk to Becky!

The only way she could think of was a very risky approach. By hovering close to the children, she would be able to absorb their heat energy as it naturally escaped their bodies. It would take a long time to build up enough energy to reveal herself, and the longer Willow stayed there, the greater the risk was of *him* finding her and punishing her.

Willow looked at the circle of salt – Becky had said that evil ghosts couldn't get past the salt. It certainly seemed to have worked with *him*. But would she, a good ghost, be able to cross it? She hovered close and moved one of her arms tentatively over the salt. Nothing happened, so she moved her whole ghostly form across it. Willow floated down, curled herself up between the chairs Becky and Finn were lying in, and waited.

After half an hour, she decided to try her luck. She moved upright and focussed on what she had to do. It had been over ten years since she had done this – she remembered now the immense concentration it took. After several attempts, she managed to bring all her collected energy together into a small orb, barely the size of a pea; she knew this wouldn't last long. Straining every ounce of her being, she blasted the ball of energy to all the particles of her ghostly form. The energy projected out of her as beams of light, casting her image into the living world.

It was a very weak image, Willow knew, but it would do. She had saved a tiny amount of energy for sound. Bending close to Becky's ear, she pushed the energy out through her mouth. It was barely a whisper, the faintest of breezes.

Willow managed 'Beck…' before her energy was gone. No more sound came and her light faded away.

She watched Becky stir slightly, turn over and go back to sleep. That proved it would work, if Willow could just build up enough energy. She curled up again, ever wary that *he* might turn up at any minute.

It was almost morning by the time she felt she had enough energy to appear to Becky properly.

Willow went through the same ritual as before, gathering all her energy together – this time the size of a large apple – and projecting it out of her body as light.

Now when she tried speaking, her voice was a lot louder.

'Becky, please wake up. I long to talk to you.'

Becky continued sleeping, so Willow repeated herself and brushed lightly against her. Becky blinked a few times and then looked straight at Willow.

'Hello,' she said. 'Who are you?'

'My name is Willow!'

She was unable to contain her excitement and flung her arms around Becky, who started to shiver. For a minute Willow thought she had made a mistake and scared Becky. She backed away.

'Sorry, I'm just very cold,' said Becky. 'Are … are you a ghost?'

'Yes.' Willow waited to see how Becky would react. Out of the few times she had tried revealing herself before, most of the people were quite scared of her. But Becky reacted in exactly the same way that Eric had – she smiled.

'You have been searching for Eric,' Willow continued.

'Yes. Do you know him?'

'I met him, ten years ago. He came to this house. I don't have long, but I would like to tell you what I know about Eric.'

Becky sat up. 'Yes, please do.'

'You may have worked out by now that Thicket House is an unusual place. Once you enter, you become trapped. You are unable to escape.'

Becky nodded.

'There are a group of us ghosts here, who were once people. We each came here, became trapped, then died. Ten years ago, Eric Pockle came to this house. Everything that has happened to you, Becky, happened to him too. He was trapped here.'

'That's what I thought. There's an evil ghost here, isn't there? That's what trapped Eric, and it's what is trapping us,' said Becky.

Willow nodded. 'Eric was an excellent ghost hunter and he came to investigate the spe—' She stopped herself saying *his* name, and settled instead for, 'to investigate the evil ghost. But Eric was also a very kind man, even when he grew weak. He found us good ghosts and grew friendly with us.'

As she spoke, Willow became aware of something closing in on her. *Him.* It had to be. She had been so excited talking to Becky that she'd forgotten to keep an eye out for the signs. She scanned the room, starting to panic.

'You said that once you enter this house, you get trapped,' said Becky. 'You have never escaped, but you speak about Eric like he isn't here any more?'

'Yes,' said Willow. *He* was very close now, hovering just the other side of the circle of salt, but she tried to smile. 'That is because Eric is the only person ever to have escaped from Thicket House.'

Becky smiled back at the ghost. 'How did he escape, Willow?'

'I can't say, Becky, not now. Just try to …

'… *get out. Eric managed, and so can you.*'

Willow looked at the expression on Becky's face. It was suddenly puzzled, her eyes searching. Willow knew what had happened – her projection had faded and Becky hadn't heard her last sentence.

Why had she faded, though? Willow had had a lot more energy left, but now it was gone. She turned around, knowing what would meet her eyes. *He* was there, in his full, terrifying form. She felt *him* sucking her out of the circle of salt.

Willow fled as fast as she could.

The Third-Floor Bedroom

When Becky woke, she saw Finn standing by the mirror above the fireplace with a blanket wrapped round him. Becky didn't really understand mirrors – she always tried to avoid looking at herself in them. Then she realised that Finn wasn't looking at his reflection; he was actually breathing on the mirror to form clouds of condensation, which he then drew in. Becky watched as he drew a fishing boat.

'Are you missing your granddad?' she asked.

Finn turned around. 'I suppose. My parents won't be worried about me – they're used to me going off fishing with Granddad for days on end. He'll be panicking about where I am, though. What about your mum?'

'She'll be worried sick that I haven't come home,' Becky admitted.

'She doesn't know you're doing this, does she?'

'There's no way she'd let me if she knew.' Becky tried to put the thought of her mum panicking out of her mind. 'Anyway, are you OK now? Did you have any more nightmares?'

Finn continued drawing his boat. 'I'm OK, I guess – still feeling a bit rubbish. I didn't have another nightmare, though. Did you?'

'No, but I met a ghost,' Becky replied.

She told him about Willow, in her long flowing dress, and what she had said about Eric escaping from Thicket House.

'Definitely a weird imagination you have,' said Finn. 'Maybe you can try dreaming us a way out of this place next time.'

'It wasn't a dream, Finn. Willow was real. I know she was.'

'Hang on. Becky, come and look at this,' Finn called her over.

'What is it?'

'Your name.'

Becky saw the writing in the latest cloud Finn had breathed on the mirror. 'You've written my name. So what?'

'No, Becky, I didn't write that.' He saw the look on her face. 'I'm not joking. It just appeared.'

'Prove it. Breathe on the mirror again.'

Finn rubbed the mirror and let out another long breath, covering the glass in condensation. Becky watched, amazed, as thick letters slowly appeared. Soon a sentence had been written.

It was not a dream.

Becky gasped. 'See, I told you Willow was real! Quick, Finn, breathe again.'

As soon as Finn had done so, more writing appeared.

Come to bedroom on third floor.

Finn rubbed this out and breathed again.

Bring wood. Light a fire there.

***

They looked up at the staircase to the third floor.

'You're right,' said Finn. 'It really is dangerous. There's no way we can get up there.'

'If Willow is real, then what she told me is also true – we're trapped in this house.' Becky scanned around nervously, expecting the shadow to appear in front of her at any moment. 'We have to go up there and ask her how Eric managed to escape.'

'But what if this Willow is just trying to trick you, to make things even worse?' asked Finn.

'This is all we have to go on, unless you have any better ideas?'

'Alright, after you then.' Finn pointed at the stairs.

Becky placed her foot on the second step, avoiding the first one that was cracked from the last time she had stood there. She looked for the strongest point in the third step and moved her other foot onto it.

'Place your feet where I place mine,' she said to Finn.

The fourth step wasn't there any more. Looking down, Becky could see through the gap the large fall to the ground floor below. She quickly looked up; the remaining steps were even worse – rotting wood, full of lightning-shaped cracks. She tested one with the lightest of touches – in a second her foot went straight through the stair and dangled in thin air under it.

'It's no good, we can't do it.'

Becky dragged her foot out of the hole.

'I know, let's try something else,' said Finn, showing enthusiasm for the first time since they had entered Thicket House.

He hopped down from the second step and disappeared downstairs. When he returned he was carrying the fire poker.

'Did you say there was a bedroom here on the second floor?' he asked.

'Through the door on your right.' Becky pointed.

She followed Finn into the bedroom, keeping alert for shadows that looked out of place, but curious about what he was planning.

Whatever his idea was, it seemed to have given him a new burst of energy. He ripped down one of the velvet curtains surrounding the four-poster bed and signalled to Becky to do the same on the other side.

'What are we using these for?' she asked.

'You'll see. We need the sheets from the bed, too.'

They pulled them off and laid the sheet and curtains on the floor.

'Can you tie knots?' asked Finn.

'No.'

'Good job my granddad's a fisherman, then – we're experts with knots.'

As she watched him hard at work, rolling the curtains and sheets into tubes, then tying them together, Becky realised what Finn was doing.

'You're creating a rope, aren't you?'

'Yep. I've used a double fisherman's knot, which will keep these sheets held together. Then if I do this …'

He threaded the fire poker into the end of the 'rope' and used another double fisherman's knot to tie it in.

'… we'll be able to throw it up the stairs and use it to climb them.'

'That's actually quite clever,' Becky admitted.

'I'm not just a pretty face.' Finn grinned.

He dragged his rope construction out to the landing and stood at the bottom of the broken staircase.

'Stand well back,' he told Becky.

Finn swung the fire poker around in the air. He let go and it flew up the stairs, carrying the long line of sheets with it. There was a thud as it landed on one of the upper steps.

'No good,' said Finn. 'I need to try and get the fire poker to stick into the floor at the top.'

He pulled it back down and tried throwing again. The same thing happened.

'You need to throw it higher,' said Becky, 'so the sharp bit of the poker lands in the floor, like it went through the door downstairs.'

So the next time Finn threw the poker, he sent it soaring into the air. It looped around and fell. The poker's point embedded itself cleanly into a floorboard at the top of the staircase. Finn pumped the air in celebration.

The rope-of-sheets attached to the poker stretched all the way down to where the children stood at the bottom of the staircase. Becky tried tugging on it and the fire poker stayed firmly in place.

'It'll take our weight.'

'Excellent!' said Finn. 'I'll go first.'

Finn placed both hands on the sheet and pressed his feet against the walls either side of the staircase. He started pulling himself up, feet not touching the steps at all. It took a while, but eventually he made it to the top.

'Now you come up,' he called to Becky. 'Do exactly what I did and don't let go of the rope.'

Becky took a deep breath and grabbed the bottom of the rope-of-sheets tightly. She lifted her legs up onto the wall and started her climb. It was easier to pull using her hands than push with her feet. She still had to concentrate on keeping her feet firmly wedged to the walls, and tried to imagine they were giant magnets. It seemed like hours by the time Becky was halfway up and she was exhausted.

She looked up at Finn – he was swaying slightly.

'You OK?' she asked.

'I'm feeling … feeling wea—' A worried expression spread over his face.

All too quickly, Becky realised why. A black shadow appeared above her. It could only be the evil ghost. It swept over her, as terrifying as a swarm of bees about to attack. She couldn't see a thing.

Balanced precariously halfway up a broken staircase, this was not the place to faint. But Becky felt like she was about to. Tentacle-like arms seemed to stretch out from the shadow and rip the energy out of her. Becky's legs shook violently as the shadow reached around them. They felt like they had turned to jelly. Becky's feet slid away from the wall, making her collapse into the staircase with a thud. The wood groaned, about to collapse.

Next the shadow surrounded her head, and she felt uncontrollably dizzy.

'Becky!'

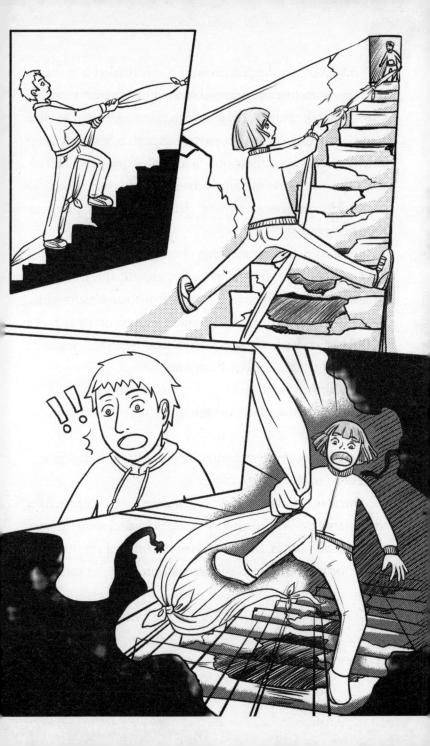

Finn's voice sounded distant, but it helped her focus. She shook her head from side to side, only just avoiding the shadow's grasp. It changed direction and went for her hands instead – the only part of her that was stopping Becky crashing to the floor below. She gripped hold of the rope-of-sheets as tightly as she could, but it was no good. Her fingers started to shake – she was about to lose her grip!

Then she felt something else. Her body slid from stair to stair, but she wasn't falling down, she was being lifted up. As Becky was released from the shadow, she saw Finn at the top of the stairs pulling her up from the other end of the rope-of-sheets. Reaching the top, Becky fell to the floor at Finn's feet.

'Thank you,' she said.

Looking back, she saw the shadow creeping up the stairs.

'That's one creepy shadow,' Finn said, backing away.

'Let's get away from it!'

The stairs had brought the children to the centre of a small landing. At the end of it, Becky saw exactly where they needed to go. She lifted herself up and ran towards the door with the sign 'Willow's Room'.

The Spectre

The room didn't seem quite as cold as the rest of the house. Becky realised she felt a lot less tense as she stepped inside.

It was simple, with a single bed, chair, wardrobe and a doll's house. Both the wallpaper and the bed sheets were covered in an old-fashioned flowery pattern. In the wall by the door was a small fireplace.

'Let's light a fire, like the writing said to. Have you got the wood?'

Finn lifted some out of the bag they'd brought from the room downstairs and placed it on the fire. Becky struck a match and watched as the wood slowly burned and a flame came to life. They waited uncertainly, expecting it to go out with a blue light. But it didn't.

'What now?' asked Finn.

'We keep waiting, I suppose.'

They sat by the fire and warmed themselves up. It was a welcome relief from the cold of the rest of the house.

'Aaahhh!' Finn cried and jumped back.

Becky looked over to see what had caused his reaction – it was a pair of pearly glasses, floating in mid-air. She blinked.

When she opened her eyes again, green eyes had appeared behind the glasses and a face around them – a young girl's face, with thick plaits hanging either side.

Finn stared, unusually amazed, as the girl's body came out of nowhere. 'Is that a ghost?'

'Hello. Please don't run away, you are safe in here – nothing can harm you,' the ghost girl said.

'Thank you. My name is Becky, and this is Finn.'

Becky had never seen a ghost so clearly before. Last night, Willow had only just been visible, but this girl glowed strongly in the light of the fire.

The girl's mouth spread into a wide grin and she spun around, her plaits dancing happily. 'It's so good to be talking to living people again! My name is Rose. We have been watching you. I heard about your fall from the chimney, Finn. Are you OK?'

'I'm fine, thanks,' Finn mumbled.

Rose turned around and spoke to thin air. 'It's alright, Peter, you can show yourself.'

The ghost of a small boy appeared – he must have

been barely six and had the eyes of a frightened rabbit. He peered cautiously at Becky and Finn from behind Rose.

'She's going to try to bottle me again, I know it!' said Peter, pointing at Becky.

'Remember that Willow said Becky didn't want to harm you,' Rose said softly. 'She just wanted to talk to a ghost.'

Seeing one ghost appear as clearly as this was unusual, but to see two floating there was so impressive that Becky's mind just seemed to accept it. Here she was having a conversation with ghosts, without needing EMF detectors, candles or anything. Finn seemed to be having the same reaction; he just sat there, staring.

'Is bottling harmful, then?' asked Becky.

'If you go in between the candles you get squished into the bottle,' said Peter. 'You get all jumbled up and confused. It's worse than death.'

'Oh, I'm sorry, Peter,' said Becky. 'I didn't realise. It doesn't say that in my ghost-hunting notebook.'

Becky pulled the notebook out of her pocket.

'That's Eric's book!' Rose exclaimed.

Becky grinned. 'You knew Eric too? Another ghost, Willow, appeared last night and told me he came to this house.'

Rose nodded, and her plaits nodded too. 'Willow lost a lot of energy last night after she talked to you. She will be here in a minute or two. She wants to tell you more about what happened when Eric was at Thicket House.'

Rose skipped over to the bed to wait; Becky and Finn followed, sitting down on the edge of the mattress. The fire's warmth went with them in a friendly glow. Peter still stayed a good distance from the two living children.

'How many ghosts are there here?' asked Becky.

'There are four of us good ghosts,' said Rose.

'But Willow said there's another ghost. A really powerful, evil one. I found it with my EMF detector yesterday.'

Peter gasped. 'She knows about *him*!'

'Have you met an evil ghost before, Becky?' asked Rose.

Becky nodded. 'My mum is the Thistlewick postmistress. The ghost of an old postmaster cursed the post office earlier this year. That was when I first started ghost hunting. It turned out that ghost wasn't completely evil, though, just angry.'

'Well, *he* is completely evil. A huge shadow that feeds off energy and will do anything to get it.'

'That's what we've seen!' said Becky. 'A shadow keeps appearing, and whenever it does, me and Finn get really weak.'

Finn nodded slowly. 'What is *he*?'

'We don't usually like to say what *he* is,' said Rose. She moved up close to Becky and Finn and whispered, '*He* is the spectre.'

Peter clasped his hands over his ears as she said it.

'I've read about spectres in Eric's ghost-hunting notebook,' said Becky. She thumbed through the notebook until she came to the right page. Peter kept his hands firmly pressed to the side of his head as she read, '"Spectres are ghosts that have never been alive and are created purely by energy. The more energy a spectre gets hold of, the more powerful it becomes and the more energy it wants. Usually tiny things that live in your attic, they occasionally take the heat from your fire or make your tea go cold, but otherwise they are harmless."'

'*He* isn't like that. *He* is the biggest, meanest spectre ever,' said Rose; her facial expression was earnest. '*He* has control over this whole house, and once *he* has trapped you, *he* won't let you escape.'

Fear flashed across Peter's face. '*He* sucks all your energy out until you die!'

'That's what happened to you ghosts, isn't it?' asked Becky.

Finn gulped. 'And it's what's happening to us. *He*'s trying to kill us!'

'But how did the spectre end up here, in a house in the middle of the forest?' Becky wondered.

'You are a very intelligent girl, Becky,' a voice said from the fireplace. A voice Becky recognised. 'You are asking all the right questions.'

Becky turned. It was Willow, but she looked different

to how she had the night before. Becky wasn't sure if ghosts could get ill, but Willow definitely looked it. Her round face was just as soft, but her ghostly appearance flickered in and out, and there were holes here and there over her body where her projection didn't come through.

'Willow, what's happened to you?' asked Peter, his mouth wide open.

'The spectre got to me.'

Peter started to put his hands over his ears again.

'Peter, we have to be brave. We mustn't be afraid to say what *he* is.' Willow turned to Becky. 'Last night, *he* caught me when I was talking to Becky and punished me for it.'

'I'm sorry, Willow, if I'd known…' Becky began.

'It's OK, Becky, I knew the risk I was taking. It's good to be talking to you again. Now, you want to know how the spectre came to be here. Let me tell you how it all started.'

Thatch

'I must stay here by the fire, if I am to keep enough energy to communicate,' said Willow.

Becky looked intently at her. Rose and Peter drifted over to the chair and floated on top of it.

'Thicket House used to be my home. This very room was my bedroom. My family had been the guardians of the forest, ever since Lord Thistlewick's time. He appointed my great-great-great-grandparents as the first guardians, and the job was passed down through the generations, until my parents became guardians. Their job was to look after the creatures and the maze of trees, and to make sure no one got lost in it. I lived here with them happily for fourteen years. But then everything changed. One day, the spectre arrived. I do not know how, or where *he* came from, but from that day our lives turned bad. It started with the heat from the stove when *he* was small, then *he* took all the heat from our fires. Eventually, as he grew, *he* moved on to us, gave us nightmares, started trapping us in rooms and taking our energy. *He* became so powerful that there was only one thing we could do – run away. So we fled the house and never returned. Or at least, my parents never did. Becky, Finn, do you ever do things against the will of your parents?'

Becky nodded. 'That's why we're here now.'

'That's your fault, not mine. I'm in this house against my own will, let alone my parents',' Finn argued.

'Like you don't do anything wrong. I always hear your granddad telling you off.'

'Well, I also disobeyed my parents,' said Willow. 'We had left Thicket House in a hurry, without any of our possessions. I wanted to come back to collect my books, my diaries and my art box – I thought I could slip back in without the spectre noticing. But my parents would not let me. We had an argument, and that night I ran back here without them knowing. It was so stupid of me – I should have listened to them. But I didn't. The second I walked through the front door I was trapped for good. I had escaped *him* once, and *he* wasn't going to let it happen a second time. Eventually the spectre took all of my energy. I died. The next thing I knew, I was trapped here as a ghost, with no one to keep me company. It was many years before the others came.'

'But this spectre still harms you, even though you're a ghost?' asked Becky.

'*He* mainly just ignores us. *He* cannot gain much energy from ghosts, so it's not worth wasting *his* own energy chasing us.'

'Why was *he* angry with you last night, then? Why did *he* waste *his* energy punishing you?'

'After I had been a ghost here for many years, I managed to make a deal with the spectre. *He* gave me my bedroom, and promised *he* wouldn't come near it, so long as I promised not to interfere with *his* business. That is why we are all safe in here now, even you living two. But last night, by talking to you, I came dangerously close to interfering and breaking my promise.'

'You're interfering now, though,' Finn pointed out.

'I know, and if the spectre finds out, *he* will be so angry with me. I dread to think what *he* would do. But I am not important, you two are. Did you understand what I told you last night, Becky?'

'You told me that Eric escaped, but you disappeared before you could explain how he did it.'

'Eric was known as a ghost hunter, but the word "hunter" seems the wrong one to use. It suggests that we ghosts were his prey, and nothing could be further from the truth. Eric was so very kind to us, and he quickly became our friend. He was also an immensely clever, special man. If anyone could find a way to get out of this place, it was him. But I do not know how he managed to escape. Only one of us saw him do it – Thatch.'

'Thatch?!' Finn exclaimed.

He looked at Becky – they both remembered the nightmare about Finn's granddad searching for his brother in the forest.

'Do you know Thatch?' asked Willow.

'I might do,' said Finn.

'Then maybe he will tell you how Eric escaped. He has always refused to tell us. Rose, have you seen that rascal?'

'He's been messing around all day in the room next door,' Rose replied.

'He was being mean to me again,' Peter said in a hurt voice. 'Pretending to be the … the … the spectre.' It took him a lot of effort to say the word he had been avoiding for over forty years, and afterwards the enormity of it seemed to leave him breathless.

'Well done, Peter, I knew you could be brave enough to say "spectre". Now, I will find Thatch and get him to appear.' Willow flickered out of sight.

A couple of minutes later, the ghost returned, dragging an arm along with her. Becky couldn't see a body attached to it.

'Don't worry,' said Willow. 'It's Thatch's arm. He always stores up lots of energy, but he's refusing to appear. I can make him show the rest of himself, but he is wriggling too much. Can someone help me hold him down?'

Rose and Peter soared over to her, looking only too glad to help. Thatch sounded to Becky like he was a mischievous ghost. After struggling for a while, the other ghosts managed to pin him down. Willow floated over him and a golden glowing ball appeared at the centre of his body. It spread over him, revealing to Becky and Finn a scruffy boy with dirty shorts and roughed-up hair.

'Becky and Finn, meet Thatch. Thatch, meet Becky and Finn,' said Willow, sounding out of breath. She moved over to the fire to warm up again.

Thatch stuck his tongue out at them all.

'You said you know Thatch?' Willow prompted Finn.

'Um … yeah, I … I think we're related. Is your surname Gailsborough?'

'How'd you know that?' Thatch asked accusingly.

Finn had an expression on his face that Becky could only describe as a 'this-is-weird-I'm-talking-to-my-granddad's-dead-brother' look.

'Albert Gailsborough is my granddad.'

Thatch's face turned very serious – almost horrified. He tried to struggle out of the other ghosts' grip.

'Becky and Finn want to know how Eric managed to escape,' said Willow. 'I know you can tell them.'

Thatch stared long and hard from Finn to Becky. With a final effort he pushed Peter away from him. The young ghost fell backwards into the fire with a scream and disappeared. Rose let go of Thatch and followed Peter to see if he was OK. Willow grabbed Thatch's arm, but her grip was weak. He freed himself easily from it and shot towards the door.

'You'll have to catch me first!'

The Spectre Attacks

Thatch shot out of the room. Finn made a dramatic, flying dive towards the door. For a moment it looked like his hand had successfully grabbed hold of Thatch's foot. But it passed straight through.

Thatch looked back with a grin as Finn slid along the floor.

Becky ran forwards, jumping over Finn. 'Get up, we've got to catch him!'

But how do you catch a ghost? she thought as she ran full pelt.

Thatch went up the landing and swerved left into a side room opposite the stairs. The door slammed shut. Becky skidded to a halt outside the room and pressed her ear to the door. She was thrown forwards as Finn fell into the back of her. Becky put her finger to her lips, signalling him to be quiet. They listened carefully.

Inside, they could hear giggling.

'Come in, if you dare,' said Thatch's voice.

Finn stepped forwards and threw the door open. Becky scanned around but there was no sign of the ghost boy. There weren't many places he could hide. He wasn't by the desk on the right, nor by the stack of rotten boxes on the left.

'Maybe he's hidden inside one of the boxes,' Finn suggested.

'Or made himself invisible,' said Becky. 'Come on, Thatch, we don't have time for this.'

'I've got all the time in the world,' a voice came from above them.

Becky and Finn looked up to see a sheet being dropped from the ceiling on to them, bringing with it a huge cloud of dust. Thatch let out a roar of laughter as the two children had major coughing fits.

Becky recovered first and swung her arms around, trying to escape from under the sheet. After getting tangled up a few times, she eventually crawled out.

Thatch was floating nearby, holding a piece of coal in his left hand.

Becky turned to look at Finn, still under the sheet, and couldn't help letting out a giggle. Thatch had drawn a big smiley face on the sheet with the coal, right where Finn's head was. The eyes of the face were pointing in different directions.

'Oi! What are you two laughing at?' Finn's voice came from under the sheet, making it look like the smiley face was talking.

His body flailed about until he managed to free himself. The expression on his face as the sheet slid away was the exact opposite of the one Thatch had drawn.

Finn glared at the ghost. 'It was you who chased us around the living room, wasn't it?'

'So what if it was?' said Thatch.

'You tried to kill me with that fire poker. You tried to kill your own relative!'

'Not kill, exactly. Just scare.'

'Can you two stop arguing?' Becky stepped in. 'Thatch, please tell us how Eric escaped.'

'No way. I'm not telling you how Eric Pockle got out. You'll just leave us here like he did!'

With one last glare to match Finn's, Thatch was gone – he'd turned himself invisible.

Becky looked around. A door in the right-hand wall of the room swung itself open.

'Through there,' said Finn.

They ran towards the door, but before they could get through, it slammed in their faces.

'The cheeky little—'

'Finn, let's go back to the landing,' whispered Becky. 'I saw a second door in the room he's just gone in, which must lead out onto the landing. I bet he's going to come out there.'

They crept out to the landing and over to the next door on the left. Finn was still holding the sheet. Becky took hold of one edge and pointed to Finn to stand the other side of the door. The sheet stretched out across the doorway, ready to catch Thatch.

'Can't ghosts just go straight through sheets?' Finn whispered.

'I don't think so. I mean, most people think they can go through walls, but they can't,' Becky replied.

As they had predicted, the door opened. But when Thatch came out, he no longer had a mischievous face – it was now stricken with fear.

'*He*'s coming,' the ghost said hoarsely. 'The spectre is up here, I can feel *him*. Run! Hide!'

The two living children paused for a second, unsure what to do. Then they fled.

Remembering the pile of boxes, Becky ran back into the room opposite the stairs and dived behind them. An icy chill flooded over the entire room and Becky felt dizzy. *He* must be close.

'Finn, in here!' she called.

Finn was in the doorway, about to run in, when another call came.

'Becky, Finn, come back to my bedroom, it's the only safe place.' It was Willow.

Finn turned, unsure which way to go. Becky shook her head. She was feeling fainter by the second.

'We don't have time,' she mouthed to Finn.

But he shot off along the landing towards Willow's room. Becky hoped he would make it. Then, a shadow swept down the landing – the shadow that had trapped her on the staircase, but darker now than any shadow Becky had ever seen. It was the spectre.

She squeezed over so she could see more of the landing. Finn had made it to the stairs, but there was too far to go to get to Willow in time. Finn turned around to face the growing shadow. He squinted his eyes and moved his hand to his head, as if the shadow was the brightest thing he had ever seen. It was just like watching Eric in her nightmare.

Becky wanted to call out to Finn, to run and help him, but she knew there was nothing she could do. The spectre was onto him.

Then the screaming started.

At first it was a low rumble. The shadow – the spectre – got blacker still and the rumble turned into a growl, then a high-pitched thunderous screech. Finn let out a scream too – Becky had never heard such fear. The sounds continued unbearably, the whole house shook, as the shadow swarmed around Finn. He went rigid, completely stiff, as sparks of energy seemed to fly from the spectre. Then, with a sudden burst of energy, all sound stopped. Everywhere was silent.

Finn swung too and fro at the top of the staircase.

Becky looked on in horror as the spectre appeared to reach around Finn and suck all his energy out. Then a tentacle-arm extended from the spectre and pushed him. Finn fell, painfully slowly, down the rotten stairs. There was a loud cracking sound, a sickening thud.

Becky gasped. It sounded like Finn had crashed down to the floor below!

Before she had a chance to react, she saw the black shadow moving into the room she was hiding in. Her gasp had shown the spectre where she was. She pressed herself down as tight as possible, waiting for the worst to happen.

But nothing did happen. She didn't feel faint or dizzy, and none of her limbs started shaking.

Becky slowly opened her eyes. She saw the spectre there, filling the entrance to the room. *His* monstrous form had forced the door to break off its hinges. But *he* just floated there. The spectre had no eyes that Becky could see, but she was sure that *he* was staring straight at her. Almost studying her.

Several long, twisted tentacles of darkness stretched out towards her. Becky braced herself. The tentacles curled around her head, which began to throb with pain as the spectre pulled something out.

But it wasn't her energy.

Becky blinked. In front of her was an image, which filled her whole vision. The image was of herself, aged

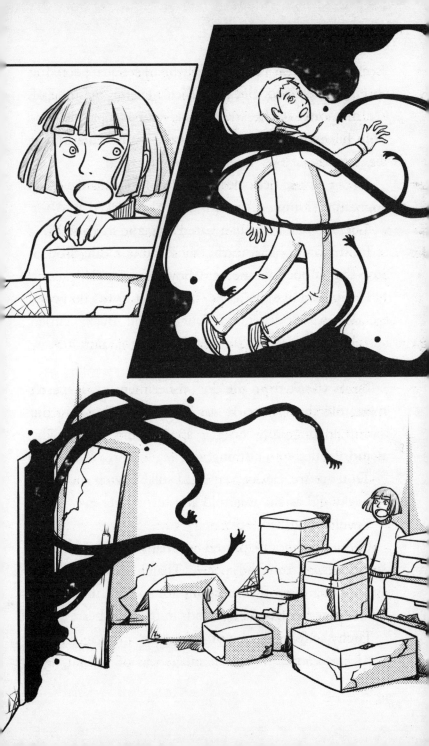

four, backing into a corner of the market square, looking absolutely terrified. Becky realised that this was one of her memories – the spectre had extracted a memory from her mind and they were watching it like a film at the cinema.

Four-year-old Becky let out a scream as a giant, vicious dog came stomping towards her. She backed into the wall behind her as the dog bared its razor-sharp teeth.

From somewhere nearby, there came a call: 'Rocco! Stop that at once! Come here, boy.'

It sounded like the dog's owner. But it was no good, the dog wasn't listening. Four-year-old Becky curled herself up, waiting for the snarling dog to attack her...

There came a roar.

But it wasn't from the dog in her memory. It wasn't even from the spectre. It was Thatch. He shot into the room, floating between the spectre and Becky. The memory faded into nothing.

'Don't move, Becky. Stay dead still,' Thatch shouted.

Becky did as she was told and turned her eyes away. She couldn't bear to look.

It felt like hours passed as many bone-shattering screams came from the spectre. Thatch sounded like he was fighting *him* off. The room got so dark that Becky couldn't see her trembling hands in front of her.

Then she felt a release of tension.

All was silent.

Snakes and Ladders

'Becky, thank goodness you're safe.'

Willow floated close to Becky as she uncurled herself.

'What ... what happened?'

'Thatch managed to stop *him* from attacking you. He got the spectre to chase after him. We're safe, for now.'

'What about Finn?' Becky sat up shakily.

'He's just lying there,' Peter said from the doorway.

'He needs your help,' said Rose.

Becky stumbled over to the staircase, where she had seen Finn fall. It was even more broken now, with bits of stair and railing sticking out dangerously. Down at the bottom in a heap of debris was…

'Finn,' Becky groaned. 'He's not…' She couldn't finish her sentence.

Willow soared down to him. She pressed her ear close to his head.

'He's breathing,' she said. 'Finn is still alive.'

Becky breathed a sigh of relief. She knew what she had to do.

She grabbed hold of the rope-of-sheets and swung down the staircase at top speed to get to Finn. He wasn't cut and nothing seemed to be broken, thank goodness, but he was in a bad way. As she tried to lift him he gave a faint moan.

'Come on, Finn, you have to help me.'

But he couldn't. He just lay there, limp. Becky had to get him to the safety of Willow's bedroom. There was no way she would have the strength to carry him up.

'Could you tie him to the sheets and pull him up from the top of the stairs?' Willow suggested.

Becky nodded. She took the end of the rope-of-sheets and tied it around Finn's hands.

'I may not know what a fisherman's knot is, but I hope this works.'

She tugged on the rope and it stayed attached to him. She tried getting his hands to grip it, and they seemed to hold on.

Becky quickly climbed back up the rope-of-sheets to the third floor. She planted her feet firmly on the ground, took hold of the sheets again and pulled with all her might.

Finn was heavy. Becky didn't know how she managed it but, centimetre by centimetre, she pulled him all the way up to the top of the stairs. She untied his hands and put his arm around her shoulder. She was then able to drag him into Willow's room.

To keep Finn warm, she tucked him up under a fleecy blanket she found on Willow's bed and added wood to the fire.

'Thatch was a hero, fighting the spectre like that. Will he be OK with the spectre chasing him?' Becky asked the ghosts.

'He may have caused the spectre to turn up in the first place, but Thatch was very brave to stop *him* getting to you,' said Willow. 'When Thatch has fought the spectre in the past he has always managed to get away eventually.'

'The spectre looked really angry this time,' said Peter.

'Yes,' Willow admitted. 'But there isn't a lot we can do to help Thatch. It won't be safe to go out of my room until we know whether he has shaken off the spectre, or…' But Willow didn't want to face the alternative.

Rose watched Finn as his chest rose and fell in shallow breaths. 'The spectre really has taken a lot of Finn's energy – he's so weak.'

'*He* is hungry. It has been a long time since *he* has been able to feast on human energy,' said Willow.

Becky grimaced – feasting on human energy sounded a horrible thing.

'How are you, Becky? Did the spectre take much of your energy?' Willow asked.

'It's really weird. I don't think *he* took any at all this time.'

'But we saw *him* attack you,' said Rose.

Becky frowned. 'The spectre didn't take my energy, but I think *he* did take one of my memories. *He* sort of pulled it out from my head, and now for the life of me I can't remember what that memory was. It's like it's been deleted from my mind.'

'I have never seen that behaviour from *him* before,' said Willow. 'Why would *he* stop taking your energy and take your memories instead?'

'I don't know,' Becky replied.

***

The younger ghosts were really worried about Thatch. Becky wanted to go out and find him, but Willow insisted it was too dangerous. She remembered that she had a games box under her bed, which might be a good way of distracting them all. Becky found it and soon they were playing snakes and ladders, ludo and other old-fashioned games at the end of the bed, while Finn slept.

It had been many years since any of the ghosts had played such human games, and snakes and ladders was definitely the favourite of Rose and Peter. Becky had to do most of the work; the young ghosts weren't as skilled at holding objects as Thatch. They could just about hold the dice, but found it hard to roll them. She did this for them, and then Rose and Peter were able to push their counters along the board.

Rose was having a run of good luck, landing on squares with ladders she could climb up every other turn. Each time she went up a ladder, Rose spun around happily. Becky wasn't sure that Peter got the idea of the game – he seemed to enjoy it most when he had to move his counter down the snakes.

'How did you end up getting trapped in Thicket House?' Becky asked Rose as she rolled a six on the dice.

Rose moved her counter up a ladder, spun around, and then a thoughtful look appeared on her face. It was obviously a long time since she had talked about it.

'I lived at a farm on the north of Thistlewick. Half Acre Farm, it was called.'

'That's where we get our milk from,' said Becky. 'Andrew Potts runs it now.'

'Andrew is my cousin!' Rose grinned. 'He was only a baby when I lived there forty years ago, with my parents and my dog, Stormy. Stormy was my bestest friend. He had a long glowing mane like a lion, but a face as friendly as a seal's. We did everything together. One day he ran off into the forest, chasing after a rabbit. My parents had warned me about that dark, scary place, but I was worried about him getting hurt, so I followed. I soon got lost. There was no sign of Stormy and I didn't know how to get back home. Then I found Thicket House. I was cold and hungry, so I went in hoping there was someone there to help. You know what happened after that.' Her voice trailed off.

'I'm so sorry, Rose,' said Becky, feeling upset for the ghost. 'And you never saw your parents or Stormy again?'

'No, I don't know what happened to Stormy, or Mummy and Daddy. I wish I could see them, just once more.'

'I wish I could see my mummy or daddy again, too,' Peter said quietly. 'I was a naughty boy. My mummy was in the market buying apples. I was running around bumping into things and she told me off. That annoyed me, so when she went to pay I thought I would be even naughtier. I ran away when no one was looking. I went into the forest. The trees were like big monsters from a storybook and I started to cry. Then I saw a light and followed it. It took me to Thicket House.'

Peter cried now. Willow came over and hugged him. Becky wasn't sure what to do, so she rolled the dice for him. It landed on four. Willow moved Peter's counter for him.

'Look,' she said. 'You landed on a snake, Peter.'

Peter stopped crying and smiled again as he made his counter fly down the snake to the bottom of the board.

Becky tried hard not to think about her mum and what she must be feeling now. She was glad that she hadn't told Mum anything about where she was going. It meant that even if Mum came looking for her, or called the police, they would be unlikely to find Thicket House and get trapped there too.

It was down to Becky to figure out how to break out of this place. She just hoped that Thatch would survive his fight with the spectre so that he could tell her how Eric had done it.

Thatch's Story

Becky looked up from Eric's notebook, which she had been scanning through for a while. 'Listen to this.'

The ghosts gathered around.

'It's on page 87, titled "Memories". Eric wrote, "I was told recently of several people in America who have suffered memory loss, thought to have been caused by an evil spirit. Eyewitness accounts tell of a ghostly presence extracting memories from their victim. I have not experienced this myself and there are not many theories to explain why an evil spirit would do such a thing. Having given the matter some thought, I would guess that memory extraction is a method used by evil spirits to take control of a person. Somehow, by clearing the person's mind of all their thoughts, I think the evil spirit can get inside their mind."'

'Is that what he was trying to do to you earlier?' asked Rose. 'Was *he* trying to control you?'

Feeling slightly uneasy about it, Becky shrugged.

Willow gave her a concerned look. 'You must try your hardest not to let *him* get to you.'

'How is Finn?' a voice said from the door.

Becky turned around. Thatch was hovering in the entrance.

Rose soared across the room towards him. 'Thatch! We've been really worried about you. What happened?'

'The spectre was angrier than I've ever seen *him*. I had to fight *him* all the way down to the cellar this time before *he* gave up,' said Thatch.

'How do you fight the spectre?' asked Becky.

'*He* doesn't like wasting *his* energy, but if I annoy *him* in the right way I can get *him* to chase me. I'm really quick, so *he* hardly ever catches me. We keep going until *he*'s lost too much energy. Then *he* goes away to gather all that energy back up again. I think I have made *him* angry, but at least I've bought us some time.'

'Well, I think Becky is torn between thanking you and calling you an idiot, Thatch,' Willow commented.

'I don't blame her.' He looked at Becky sheepishly. 'Sorry I made the spectre turn up and attack Finn.'

'It's obvious that you and Finn are related. You both act like idiots sometimes.' Becky sat down next to Finn on the bed. 'But thank you for saving me from the spectre, Thatch. Finn's doing OK, we think. He hasn't said anything yet.'

'He'll get better soon, I know he will. Us Gailsboroughs are strong.'

The tension in the room soon eased.

'Earlier, Rose and Peter told me how they got trapped in Thicket House,' said Becky. 'How did it happen to you, Thatch?'

'I was playing with my brother,' he replied, moving over to the fire.

Becky nodded. 'You were playing hide-and-seek, weren't you?'

'Yes. How do you know that?'

'Finn had a nightmare about it.'

'Albert was two years older than me and very sensible, so he set the rules. We could hide all over the island, but not in any caves or in the forest. We played hide-and-seek a lot, and Albert always managed to find me really quickly. This time, I decided to break the rules and hide in the forest – he'd not dare go in there, so he would never find me. I waited for what seemed like hours, until I got bored of standing in the forest. My curiosity got too big and I went further in, off the safe track. I found Thicket House and got trapped here.'

'Albert did come looking for you in the forest, though. Finn saw it in his nightmare. Albert searched for hours and hours,' said Becky.

'Oh.' Thatch's face fell. His tough exterior was melting away, revealing a sad, lonely child. 'I was so stupid, and it must have made him feel awful. I just wish that I could have said sorry to Albert.'

'I can tell him for you,' said a voice from the bed.

Becky turned to look at Finn. He was sitting up, staring around.

'Finn, thank goodness you're OK.' Without thinking, Becky flung her arms around him and gave Finn a hug.

'Er … thanks,' he said.

Becky quickly let go and sat there awkwardly. For the first time, she noticed the pattern on the fleece wrapped around Finn.

'Flowers suit you.' She grinned.

'Oi!'

'It's good to have you back, Finn,' said Willow.

Finn looked to Thatch. 'Albert's my granddad, so I can tell him whatever you want me to. But to do that, we'll have to escape from this place.'

'Please, Thatch, can you tell us how Eric got out of here?' Becky asked again.

The ghost fidgeted nervously and didn't reply.

'Thatch.' Willow gave him a warning stare. She explained to Becky, 'He thinks that Eric broke a promise he made to us.'

'What did he promise?' asked Becky.

'Before he escaped he said he had a way to get rid

of the spectre and free us all,' said Thatch. 'That was his promise – to free us, so that Rose, Peter and Willow could see their parents again, and I could see my brother. But he escaped and left us all here.'

'I knew Eric,' said Willow. 'I know that if he could have helped us, he would have done.'

'No!' Thatch shouted. 'He wouldn't have. When he escaped, he just went back home and never thought about us again. Never thought about our families. Just because we're ghosts doesn't mean we don't have feelings. Why should he go home when I can't? And why should Finn and Becky?'

'Thatch,' Becky said softly, remembering the reason she had come on this adventure in the first place. 'I don't think Eric did return home. Look.'

She showed him where Eric's name was written on the 'Ghosts Seen On Thistlewick' page of his notebook.

'This was found in the forest, with his name written there,' Becky explained. 'He must have died somewhere in the forest. I think Willow's right. I don't know a lot about Eric, but from what I've been told he cared more about ghosts than he did about living people. He would have done all he could to help you.'

'Please, Thatch,' said Finn. 'As your great nephew, or whatever I am, don't let what happened to you happen to Becky and me. You know how powerful the spectre is, and you've seen what *he*'s done to us already. Granddad lost his brother – don't let him lose his grandson too. Help us escape, before it's too late.'

There were a few seconds of tense silence. Everyone stared at Thatch.

'OK, I'll tell you how Eric did it,' he finally said.

Escape Plan

'When Eric came to Thicket House, he knew there was an evil ghost here,' Thatch began.

'That's what Mayor Merryweather said. It was going to be his last big investigation before he retired,' Becky remembered.

'When he realised exactly what it was, Eric tried different ways to capture the spectre. When he first came, he tried to bottle *him*, but the spectre was far too powerful for that. Eric nearly ended up bottling me, instead, a bit like you two did.'

'Sorry,' Becky said again.

'It's OK. I chased you through the living room, so we're even on that one. After that, Eric did lots of chanting around all the different rooms and used a tape recorder to see if the spectre would talk back to him.'

'He was using EVP,' said Becky. 'Electronic voice phenomenon.'

'That was when Eric found us ghosts, wasn't it?' said Willow. 'When he used his tape recorder in my bedroom. Then we all tried something that involved standing in a circle and asking the spectre to leave Thicket House.'

'That's called a Calling,' said Becky.

'Oh, like we did with the post office ghost,' Finn remembered.

'None of it worked, though,' said Thatch. 'The spectre wasn't having any of it. By that time *he* had drained a lot of Eric's energy and Eric was getting very weak. Then, one night, Eric came up with a final plan to get rid of the spectre and escape. Without telling any of us ghosts he slipped out of Willow's room. I was the only one who saw him go, so I followed, keeping well out of the way so that I couldn't be seen.'

'Where was he going?' asked Finn.

'To the ice well.'

'The ice well? Where's that?' asked Becky.

'You've been in it,' Thatched replied.

'Have I?' Becky frowned – she couldn't remember any rooms with ice in them.

'The room through the cellar with the round ceiling,' Thatch explained.

'But that room just had lots of straw in it.'

'You didn't see what was under the straw, Becky.'

'Ice,' said Willow. 'Under that straw are big slabs of ice. When I lived here there was no other way of keeping food cold. The ice well was created so that we could have a permanent supply of ice to use. Each winter, when the ponds froze over, we would cut the ice out and carry it into our ice well, where it was cold enough for the ice to stay frozen. The straw is there to insulate it.'

'But I don't understand,' said Becky. 'How could Eric get rid of the spectre by going to the ice well?'

'Think about it,' said Thatch. 'Where do ghosts get their energy from?'

'Humans, fire, hot stuff,' said Finn. Becky nodded.

'So what do you think ghosts fear?' Thatch continued.

'Er…' Finn thought. 'Getting a cold?'

'Not getting a cold – being cold!' Becky exclaimed.

'Exactly,' said Thatch. 'Heat gives us energy, but being cold takes it away from us. We all fear the cold, but the spectre fears it more than the rest of us.'

'Why?'

Thatch looked to Willow for help.

'We ghosts still have souls, the part of us that made us who we were when we were alive. Even if we lose most of our energy, we still won't quite disappear – our souls will be left, and they can collect energy again and rebuild us,' Willow explained. 'But the spectre doesn't have a soul. *He* was never a living being. That means *he* needs heat energy to survive.'

'When all *his* energy is gone, the spectre is destroyed,' said Thatch.

'So to defeat the spectre, we just have to trap *him* in the ice well?' asked Finn.

Willow shook her head. 'No, that doesn't work. When I was alive, I tried to trick the spectre into going into the ice well.'

'I tried too,' said Rose. 'It's impossible – *he* won't go near it.'

'I don't get it, Thatch,' said Willow. 'Eric can't have escaped like that. Like Rose said, it's impossible. Anyway, the spectre would have been destroyed if *he* got trapped in the ice well, and *he*'s still here.'

'Eric seemed to have a different idea about how he could use the ice. Anyway, in the end, that wasn't how he got out,' said Thatch.

'Then how did he escape?' asked Becky.

'He encouraged the spectre to chase him down to the cellar. It was horrible to watch – Eric was exhausted. He tripped over, fell down stairs, kept collapsing, and all the time the spectre was after him. But eventually, Eric made it to the cellar and was nearly at the door to the ice well. Then the spectre got too close. I thought Eric was done for. The spectre towered over him. But they just stared at each other for ages. I don't know how he did it, but Eric must have convinced the spectre to let him go, because after that Eric just turned around and walked away. He walked straight past me and out through the front door. He escaped and never returned, leaving us here with the spectre.'

'But Eric was nice. Why would he do that?' Peter asked in a small voice.

'There must be a reason,' said Becky.

'Maybe when he escaped he was going to fetch other people to help destroy the spectre, but he never made it back to the main part of Thistlewick,' Finn suggested.

'Why did Eric not tell us how he planned to escape?' asked Willow. 'He was so weak when he tried to get out. We could have helped him, but he refused to say anything.'

'He said he wanted to protect us,' said Thatch. 'He said he didn't want us to know anything, so that the spectre couldn't blame us and hurt us if it went wrong. But I think Eric didn't tell us so he could escape without us knowing.'

'Why would the spectre just let him go, though?' asked Rose.

Thatch shrugged. Then he froze. 'Did you feel that, Willow?'

She nodded. 'The spectre is close by again. *He* has gathered all *his* energy back.'

Peter started shaking and put his hands over his ears. Rose went over to reassure him.

A determined feeling was rising up inside Becky. 'I'm

going to find a way to destroy the spectre and free all of us. Not just Finn and me, you ghosts as well. I can't promise that I'll be able to do it, but I will try. Do you believe me, Thatch?'

Thatch hesitated for a minute. 'I hope so.'

'Then I need to figure out how Eric was planning to escape using the ice well. I need to get inside it and have a look.'

'You can do that on one condition.' Thatch moved over to her. 'You're not doing it alone. The spectre is waiting out there. Waiting for you to move so that *he* can attack. Even if Eric broke his promise, I let him fight the spectre on his own and it was horrible. I won't let the same happen to you. I will help you to get to the ice well.'

'I will too,' said Willow.

'We'll fight!' Rose and Peter said together.

'Right, are we going now, then?' Finn asked, rising out of the bed.

'You're not coming, Finn,' said Becky. 'Peter, you must stay here with Finn and make sure he doesn't leave this room.'

'But I want to fight,' Peter protested.

'Peter, you must be brave again,' Willow said in a motherly tone. 'Making sure Finn is safe in here is the most important thing you can do. You can play snakes and ladders with him.'

Peter nodded.

'But Becky, I—' Finn began.

'You're too weak to face the spectre again,' she told him. 'I don't want anything bad to happen to you. You need to stay here in Willow's room, where you're safe.'

Finn bit his lip, fighting back his natural instinct to protest. 'Fine.'

Becky breathed in deeply. 'So the spectre will be waiting to get us?'

'I would bet my life on it, if I had one,' said Thatch.

Becky delved into her bag and pulled lots of things out, throwing them on the floor, until she came to a small electric fan.

'Rose, can you hold this?'

Rose took it from Becky. It was the heaviest thing she had ever tried to hold as a ghost. At first she couldn't manage to focus her energy on the fan and it fell to the floor. Becky picked it up and Rose had another go. She concentrated every ounce of energy on it, until the fan floated in her hands.

'When you press the button and the blades turn, a cold breeze will come out of it. You can use that to scare the spectre away.'

Rose pressed the button. When the fan turned on it was facing towards her. The breeze blew straight through her, making her image go pale as some of her heat energy was replaced by cold. She let out a small shriek and hurriedly turned it off.

'It definitely works,' she said.

Becky handed Willow a bottle of water. 'This is really cold. Throw the water at the spectre when he gets too close.'

Willow took hold of the bottle, careful to hold it by the lid, rather than the sides the cold water lay against.

Becky searched her bag again but couldn't find anything to give Thatch.

'Do you think you'll be able to fight the spectre again, Thatch? You did it so well last time.'

'Of course,' Thatch said confidently.

'Right. Let's get to the ice well!'

Becky smiled at Finn, then walked out of the safety of Willow's bedroom.

The Chase

In the gloom it was hard to tell what was shadow and what was just darkness. Becky's senses were on full alert, prepared for the spectre to appear from anywhere.

But the third-floor landing was surprisingly calm and empty – the only shadow was her own. She climbed down the rope-of-sheets to the second floor with ease now, Willow, Rose and Thatch following closely behind.

Becky reached the stairs that led to the ground floor and was about to climb down them, when…

'Becky!' called Thatch.

She swung around and saw a dark mass shoot out of the bedroom, blocking her from the ghosts. Becky froze, unable to move at the edge of the staircase. As *he* drew closer, the spectre seemed to crackle with energy. *His* shape was sharp and pointed. He really was angry! She tried to scream but no noise came out as the spectre shot around her. It got darker and darker and Becky was blinded by the intense blackness. Her head throbbed. It felt like it was being torn open as memories flashed in front of her...

There she was, with her best friend, Jimmy. They were only five and it was the first time they had met. Their mums chatted on a bench while they played on the swings, pretending to be astronauts soaring into space...

More memories flashed by: Becky and Jimmy's first day at school; their first argument after she broke his model space rocket; the day Jimmy twisted his ankle falling off his bike and Becky carried him to the doctors'...

No, Becky thought, *you can't take my memories of Jimmy. Please don't!*

Just then, she felt her legs moving backwards towards the stairs – she tried to pull them back, but they wouldn't respond.

'Becky, be careful!' she heard Willow shout.

But there was nothing Becky could do – she had no control over her legs, or the memories that were now zooming past her at a magnificent rate, each one remembered then quickly forgotten. Finally the spectre reached her memories from a few weeks before...

Becky and Jimmy were in the spare room of her flat, with Spooky Steve the ghost hunter. The ghost of Walter Anion appeared and threw Steve to the floor. He turned on Jimmy and stared menacingly down at him. Then Jimmy started to fade out of the memory...

From outside it, Becky stretched her arms towards her friend, desperate to stop him from leaving her mind. But her arms were quickly pinned down by her side by some invisible force.

Her memories vanished. The darkness cleared. Free from the spectre's grasp, Becky gasped. Her body unfroze and flopped. Off balance, she swayed back and forth.

From nowhere, the spectre appeared again. She watched as *he* spun *him*self into an intense black ball. Becky felt her mouth opening as the ball fired towards her, like it was being shot out of a cannon. *He* was aiming for her head – for her open mouth. But the spectre hadn't aimed well enough, and instead collided with Becky's stomach. Becky barely felt the impact as *he* sent her flying down the stairs.

Except she didn't fall. Suddenly, she was floating in the air, perfectly still. At the top of the stairs she saw Rose with the fan. She was waving it at the black ball of the spectre – and it worked. The ball started to disintegrate. With a piercing scream the spectre vanished. Becky felt a huge sense of relief, but she was still floating in mid-air. Had time stopped momentarily? Would it now start again and send her crashing to the bottom of the stairs? She waited, and nothing happened. What had stopped her falling?

She looked down and saw Willow and Thatch, all their energy focussed on holding her up.

'Thank you,' she breathed as they stood her upright on the top step again.

'Well done, Rose,' said Willow, hugging the young ghost. 'The spectre was trying to knock you down the stairs, Becky.'

Becky's body tensed in realisation. 'No, *he* wasn't trying to knock me down. *He* was taking my memories again. Ask me who my best friend is.'

'Who's your best friend?' asked Thatch.

'I don't remember!' Becky exclaimed. 'The spectre has just wiped all my memories of my best friend out of my head. And I think Eric's theory is right – I'm sure the spectre is trying to control me, to get inside my head.'

'I really have never seen the spectre do that before,' said Willow.

'I think I have,' Thatch said gravely. 'The expression on your face just then, Becky, when *he* was taking your memories, was the same as the expression Eric had when he walked out of Thicket House and left us all here. You had a sort of dead look in your eyes, and so did he.'

'Do you think the spectre tried to get inside Eric's head too?' asked Rose.

'I don't know, but run! *He*'s back again!' called Thatch.

Sure enough, the shadow was re-forming in front of them.

Becky clenched her fists and followed the ghosts down the stairs and into the hexagonal room with the big vase.

'We must stop the spectre getting anywhere near Becky,' Willow said to the other ghosts.

Becky ran to the door leading to the kitchen and tugged on the handle. 'It won't budge – it's wedged shut. I thought I'd left it open.'

'The spectre will have made it extra tight,' said Thatch. 'After you found the ice well so easily before, *he*'s making it difficult for you to get in there again.'

Becky started to sway. '*He*'s in this room somewhere.'

Willow looked around. 'I can feel *him* too, but I cannot see *him*. Focus on getting into the kitchen, Becky.'

'I need something to lever the door open.'

Becky rummaged through her bag and found a pencil that would be thin enough to fit in the gap between the door and the doorframe. She shoved it in and pulled it.

The ghosts all sensed the spectre now. Rose held out her fan, Willow her water, Thatch his fists.

'You can do it, Becky,' said Willow.

'Come on!' Becky gritted her teeth. All her force was on the pencil. She could feel it breaking. It snapped and flew to the floor.

She bent down to pick it up and saw the vase vibrating.

'The spectre's in the vase!'

'Why's *he* in there?' asked Rose.

'To stop you from blowing the fan at *him*, maybe.'

'Don't let *him* get to you,' Willow reminded her.

The ghosts packed round Becky tightly, but it was no good. As the vase vibrated it lifted off the floor and flew up in front of Becky.

Her vision flicked off like a light switch and now she saw a memory of the post office in front of her – the spectre's next target.

'No!' Becky screamed. 'I won't let you in.'

But the memory of the post office got stronger and clearer. Becky saw her mum through the window, serving a customer in the main shop. Then…

A cry snapped her out of the memory. Becky watched as Willow moved up behind the floating vase and opened the bottle of water. She sent it flying into the vase. A warm, rancid smell came out of it, almost like *he* was burning up. Bubbling sounded from inside the vase, turning into a great fizzling roar as *he* shot out of it and over to the other side of the room, sparks flying from *him*.

The vase hovered in the air for a second, then crashed to the floor, smashing into pieces.

'Well done, Willow, that's held *him* back,' said Thatch. 'Quick, Becky, we don't have long.'

Becky looked at the smashed pieces of vase on the floor and grabbed the biggest piece. It was sharp and pointy. She plunged it into the gap of the door and pulled. The door opened slightly, just enough for her to get a proper grip on it. She pulled and pulled until the door creaked open.

Becky and the ghosts fell into the kitchen, but not in time. They felt *his* darkness creep in behind them.

17

Flying Cutlery

'The door at the end, Becky, that's where you've got to go,' Thatch urged.

The thin kitchen seemed much longer than it had the last time Becky was in it. The door at the other end felt like it was many miles away.

Becky focussed on it – the small, wooden door – all that stood between her and the cellar steps.

She ran.

'The spectre's furious,' Rose called.

Becky looked back just in time to see the cupboards behind her fly open. As *he* chased after her, *he* sent glasses, plates and cutlery soaring out of the cupboards. They all collided with each other and smashed with many crashes.

He was trying to frighten her, but she wouldn't let

him. Becky covered her face with a hand to protect it from bits of plate that had bounced off a stray knife.

'*He*'s desperate to get to you,' Willow replied.

Becky was halfway to the cellar door.

She looked back to the part of the kitchen she had come from. It was completely black, the spectre filling the whole kitchen. She could no longer see her ghost friends, just *him*.

Memories started to flicker in front of her and Becky knew at once it had been a mistake to look at the spectre. *He* had found a way back into her mind.

'Run, Becky, run!' called Thatch.

But she couldn't. She was paralysed as images flashed through her mind. Images of school, of night-time campfires, of going out fishing with Finn, all jumbled up and confused, then instantly forgotten.

Becky felt something brush against her.

'It's Willow. Be brave, Becky. Be strong. Fight against *him*. Don't let *him* in.'

'It's so hard…' Becky mumbled. It felt like a thousand thunderclaps were going off in her mind. She felt sick.

'I know. You are so close, though, Becky. So close to the ice well,' Willow whispered.

Behind the noise of the spectre's screams and banging, Becky could faintly hear what was going on, and it didn't sound good.

Thatch said in a cracked voice, 'Rose, use the fan before *he* gets too close to Becky.'

Rose panicked. 'It's … it's not working. *He* must have sucked all the energy out of it.'

Becky's memory of every nightmare she had ever had appeared in front of her. The pirates and monsters and demons from her dreams flashing by in seconds. It terrified her. *He* was wiping her mind far more quickly now and it was excruciating.

Becky closed her eyes. She didn't know what to do.

'Becky?' Willow asked, concerned.

The spectre was getting closer. *He* was too powerful, like a steel nail hammering into Becky's head.

'Thatch, do something, stop *him*!' called Willow.

'I'm on it,' he called back.

Becky shook her head violently, trying to force the spectre out. She felt her legs walking her back towards the spectre. No matter how hard she tried, she couldn't stop them. *He* was in full control of them.

But suddenly, Becky's eyes cleared. Her legs stopped moving and she collapsed to the ground. Looking up, she saw again what was happening around her. The spectre no longer covered the whole room, only a small area around which Thatch was whizzing, clattering pans and plates. Somehow he was distracting the spectre.

'Now is your chance, Becky,' said Willow.

Becky turned round and ran full pelt into the door to the cellar. It burst open and she hurtled down the steps. Out of the corner of her eye, she saw something following her – a great number of things, in fact. She reached the bottom of the steps and turned. At least ten knifes were flying straight at her, sent by the spectre, like a group of hungry seagulls fighting to get the same fish.

Becky backed into the wall at the bottom of the steps. She screwed up her eyes as the knives got nearer and nearer.

But the spectre hadn't just thrown them at her – *he* was still in full control of them. None of the knives hit her; instead they plunged into the wall around her, some catching her hair, others going straight through the edge of her clothes, pinning her to the wall.

At the top of the steps, the spectre appeared, larger than life. Thatch obviously hadn't been able to hold *him* off for long. In a flash *he* was in front of Becky, towering over her.

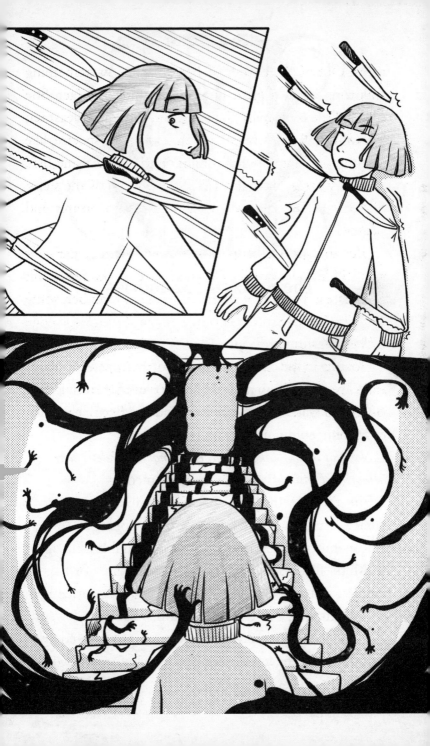

The Spectre's Memories

Becky's heart turned to ice.

Floating in the darkness in front of her was a memory of Mum. A memory Becky hadn't even realised she had. Mum was tucking a bib around toddler-Becky and feeding her some mashed-up banana.

No! Not Mum! Take any other memory, but don't take my memories of Mum! Becky's mind screamed.

But the spectre sent an uncountable number of tentacle-arms flying at her, each one ripping memory after memory out of Becky. It was unbearable as images of Mum flashed by ten times faster than normal, a hundred times, a thousand. Becky fought to remember who Mum was, but as the memories came and went, what she remembered about her mum got blurred and confused. She knew it wouldn't be long before she would have no memories of Mum left.

Six-year-old Becky was helping Mum deliver the post, then Mum was cutting seven-year-old Becky's hair, then she was telling an eight-year-old Becky off for going rock-climbing without permission.

As Becky watched the memories disappear, tears streamed from her eyes. How was she ever meant to get out of this house? She was trapped by an evil spectre. *He* was taking her memories. She could see *him* there, watching, waiting until her mind was empty enough to get inside and take control. All Becky's fight and determination was slipping away; her bright blue eyes were fading. She wanted Mum there now, to hug and comfort her, tell her it would be OK. But Mum wasn't there, and soon she would be forgotten, forever.

Becky didn't know where it came from, but somehow she found the strength to scream out, 'NOOOOO! I WON'T LET YOU IN!'

This seemed to surprise the spectre. *He* stopped for a second, and the memory in front of Becky – of Mum tucking her into bed – paused.

Then Becky had a thought. If the spectre was taking her memories, could she reach into *his* mind and take *his*? There was no way of knowing if this was possible, or if the spectre even had a mind and memories to take. But she had to do something to stop *him*.

Becky stared through the darkness to where she

thought the centre of the spectre was. She tried to imagine a giant claw reaching in and scraping out *his* mind.

But there was only darkness.

Then, an image flickered, in between Becky and the spectre – small and faint at first, but it grew bigger. It was an image she hadn't seen before – not one of her memories. She was looking down at a girl, a man and a woman eating dinner around a table. They were sitting in the hexagonal room and Becky recognised the girl as a younger Willow. The man – her father – was telling the woman – her mother – about the giant vase he had just brought back from the market.

'We can grow a sunflower in it,' he said.

Becky looked over to the vase, which was by one of the walls. She watched as a small black dot floated out of it. If she hadn't been looking for it, she would never have seen it. It was the spectre, but from when *he* was new and tiny.

'So that's how you got inside Thicket House,' Becky said.

She looked deeper into the spectre and found another memory. This was working – Becky was taking the spectre's memories and *he* had stopped taking hers. *He* was struggling against her, but she wouldn't let *him* pull away – not now she was in control.

A new image flickered in front of her. Willow's mother was trying to light the stove in the kitchen. Becky saw the spectre zoom down. Every time the woman lit a match, the spectre took its heat. Becky didn't just see the image this time; she felt the buzz of energy each time the spectre gained more heat; she heard *him* laughing to *him*self; she sensed *him* growing.

As Becky concentrated hard on the spectre, digging even further in, the memories started going by faster. In each memory she saw *him* getting bigger, and Willow and her parents getting weaker and more scared. *He* took their fires, gave them nightmares, started shutting them in rooms, and became a huge swirling mass of darkness.

Eventually, they decided to leave the house. Becky watched Willow's father running from room to room, gathering up what possessions he could hold. The spectre, now almost the size *he* was today, was chasing after him, sucking away his energy.

Becky heard a low whisper: *I take man's energy. I make him weak. I grow strong!*

With a shock, she realised she was listening to the spectre's thoughts. They made the hairs on the back of her neck prickle.

In the hallway, Willow was arguing with her mother. She wanted to go upstairs to get her art things, but her mother wouldn't let her. As they went to the front door, the spectre tried to take control of it, to force it shut.

I trap the humans here, Becky heard *him* think.

But *he* wasn't quite strong enough yet to keep the

thick front door locked. Willow's father wrenched it open with a hammer and they escaped. Becky watched the spectre explode and felt *his* scream of anger.

She moved quickly past the next series of memories – of Willow sneaking back into Thicket House, then Thatch, Peter and Rose. She knew what had happened to them, and didn't want to watch the spectre's joy in taking their energy. But then she found a memory of Eric and clawed this out to look at.

In the black space between Becky and the spectre, the image appeared. Eric, the ghost hunter with the thick-rimmed glasses twitching on his nose, was running down the stairs from the third floor. She recognised what was happening from Thatch's description. This was after Eric had promised the ghosts he would free them, when he had tried to get to the ice well. Now Becky would find out what had happened when the spectre caught up with Eric.

Thatch was right. It had been a struggle for Eric to get to the cellar. Becky soared along with the spectre as *he* forced Eric to fall down the stairs. Eric stumbled, the spectre slammed doors in his face. By the time Eric reached the cellar, he dropped down in exhaustion. As he clambered towards the door to the ice well, the spectre shot up to him.

Old man tired, the spectre thought. *I take all his energy!*

'No, please, no!' Eric called out.

Becky held her breath. This was the moment Thatch had described, where Eric had convinced the spectre to let him escape from the house. What had Eric said?

But he said nothing. As Eric tried to get away from the spectre, his notebook fell out of his pocket and opened on a page.

Page 87 – Memories.

The spectre saw the page before Eric hurriedly picked the book up and thrust it back in his pocket.

Thoughts now fired through *his* mind rapidly. Page 87 had given *him* an idea.

Not much energy left to take from old man… Not much left in whole house… But I big now… I can use old man… His book says I can take his memories, go inside him, take control!

This was clearly a thought the spectre had not had before and it excited *him*.

I use old man's body to get to new house, with new energy!

Becky felt the shiver that ran through the spectre's whole being. In an instant, Eric stopped panicking – his body swayed, limp, and his eyes looked empty. The spectre had hypnotised him.

'Is this what you are trying to do to me, too?' Becky asked.

Next, the spectre reached into Eric's mind and pulled at it with a great force. All his memories seemed to come out at once and Eric slumped down with a faint cry.

While Eric was so weak, the spectre split *him*self in two. Becky felt the big electric crack of energy that ran through *him* as it happened. It was just like bacteria, which Becky remembered being told about at school. To begin with there was just one bacteria; this split in half to make two bacteria, which split again to make four. It continued until there were hundreds and thousands of bacteria, which had all come from that one original bacteria. Or in this case, Becky realised with a horrified feeling, hundreds of spectres.

One half of the newly-split spectre stayed in the cellar, but the other half zoomed straight into Eric's mouth. Eric was knocked to the floor as the big, black shadow disappeared inside him. He slowly staggered up, and Becky knew it was no longer Eric controlling the body, but the spectre. She could feel *him* inside, laughing with glee.

Becky knew what *his* plan was now. *He* was going to walk Eric's body out of Thicket House and find a new house. If it worked, *he* could do it again, and again, and soon the spectre would take over every house on Thistlewick Island!

Eric's body flailed about for a minute as the half of the spectre inside him learnt how to control it. Then, Eric slowly walked out of the cellar. Although separated, both parts of the spectre still seemed to share the same mind, as Becky was able to see this memory through both of them. The spectre found Eric's body hard to control – the legs wobbled and crashed into the steps painfully, but Eric had no expression on his face. His body proceeded through the kitchen, where Becky noticed Thatch in the corner. He floated up to Eric and started to plead with him, but the spectre ignored Thatch and made Eric's body walk past. Out in the hallway, the spectre raised Eric's hand to the front door, which opened. The old man stepped out.

The spectre's thoughts were almost unbearable to listen to. *He* was overjoyed at the thought of taking over another house and spreading *his* power across Thistlewick.

But Becky quickly sensed that something was wrong. Eric's body was only a few hundred metres away from the house when it started to shake. The old ghost hunter was too weak to survive the trek back through the forest, especially with his mind erased and the spectre overpowering him. The spectre desperately tried to keep control of Eric's limbs, but it was no good. The legs gave way, the body collapsed to the ground.

Eric lay there, lifeless.

Becky saw the part of the spectre that had been inside the body ease out. As the black mass appeared, *his* arms flailed about as *he* was picked up by a forest breeze and blown around in the cold air until that part of the spectre was no more.

The part of the spectre still in Thicket House felt what had happened. Becky sensed the rage building up in *him*. *He* let out the biggest scream Becky had ever witnessed. It shook the floors and the walls. The whole house vibrated.

As the image faded, Becky realised that the screaming wasn't just coming from inside *his* memory. The spectre, in front of Becky now, was screaming too. *He* pulled his tentacle-arms away and shot back up the steps away from her.

By taking *his* memories, she had scared the spectre off, at least for now.

The Ice Well

Becky pulled herself off the wall she had been stuck to. She didn't care that her clothes ripped where knives had gone through them.

'Quick, ask me about my mum,' she said when Willow and Rose appeared.

'What is her job?' Willow replied.

'She's the Thistlewick postmistress.'

'What colour hair does she have?' asked Rose.

'She's got brown hair, like mine but darker, and brown eyes to match. And I love her! Oh, thank goodness, the spectre didn't manage to wipe her out of my head.'

Thatch joined them. 'I think you've scared *him* off. How did you do it?'

Becky quickly explained, then said, 'Thatch, Eric didn't break his promise to you.'

'I knew it!' Willow beamed.

'He really was trying to get to the ice well and find a way to destroy the spectre. I saw it in the spectre's memories. Eric was right in his notebook – evil ghosts do take your memories in order to empty your mind and gain control over you. That's exactly what happened to Eric. He was no longer in control of his own body when he went past you.'

Thatch hung his head. 'I am a fool. Why didn't I trust him?'

'Is that what the spectre has been doing to you, Becky?' asked Willow.

'It must be. *He* wants to move to a new house. That's why *he*'s trying to get inside my head – so he can use my body to multiply and go somewhere else.'

A roar came from the top of the steps that made them all jump.

'I can't let the spectre spread around Thistlewick. I have to destroy *him*, and the way to do it must have something to do with the ice well. If only I can get *him* to go in there.'

Thatch tensed. 'Quick, *he*'s coming back!'

Becky ran full pelt towards the metal door to the ice well and heaved it open. A cold blast hit her. The ghosts fled and hid in the fireplace as a dark mass appeared at the other end of the cellar. Blue sparks flew off *him* as *his* shape became spiky again.

'Spectre! Come in here with me,' Becky called. 'I'll let you take all my memories if you do.'

But the spectre didn't move – *he* knew that it was a trick. If *he* got too close to the ice it would make *him* weak.

'There has to be some way of getting the spectre into the ice well,' Becky said desperately.

'Just get inside and close the door,' Thatch urged her. 'Once you're in there you're safe from *him*. Then you'll have time to think of a plan. We'll hold the spectre off.'

Becky nodded. 'Make sure Finn's OK. Don't let the spectre attack him again.'

'I'll keep my great-nephew safe!' said Thatch. 'Now go!'

Becky smiled at the ghosts and closed the door, shutting out the spectre's screams.

In the pitch black, she rummaged in her bag for the torch. It wasn't there – she must have left it upstairs. Becky felt her way along the short tunnel, the cold increasing as she went, until she came to the domed room of the ice well. She stepped forwards until her feet found straw. She pressed down on it carefully – if this was an ice well, that might mean there was a large hole in the ground, which Becky could fall down if she wasn't careful. Whatever was under the straw, though, it was solid. As Becky put more weight on it, there was a breaking sound. It was the ice.

Her foot slipped as the piece of ice that had broken dislodged itself. She tried to pull her leg away, but it was too late. Off balance, she tripped, fell forwards onto the straw and was plunged through it.

Becky bounced off sharp-edged pieces of ice, her arms and legs cracking them as they went. She landed with a gasp in the middle of all the ice. It wasn't a gasp of pain, though – Becky was shocked at the sudden drop in temperature. It was clear why a ghost couldn't survive in the ice well; even if she was attempting the world record for the most jumpers worn in one go, Becky would still be shivering from the iciness.

Her body reacted by trying to escape the ice, but as soon as she jumped up, she just slid back down, frozen still. It wasn't exactly a well in the way she thought it would be; it felt more like she was sitting amongst ice in a giant's cereal bowl. Unable to see exactly what was around her, she swung her arm up. It brushed against thin, small pieces of ice and bigger, thick pieces. She found one that was big enough to take her weight and grabbed hold of the top of it with both hands. The ice was so cold that if she left her hands touching it for too long she was sure they would drop off from frostbite. Her experience of climbing the rocks around Thistlewick came in handy as she pulled herself up. She found a ledge of ice to place her feet on and, with a great effort, heaved herself out of the ice well.

Becky stood up, her eyes adjusting to the darkness again, and started to think of how she could use the ice to get rid of the spectre. What had Eric been planning to do?

If the spectre had no control over this room, could she break through one of the walls to escape? To get Willow and the others out, she could bottle them to protect them from the icy chill of the well and stick them in her pocket. But that wouldn't destroy the spectre – it wouldn't stop anyone else coming to the house and getting trapped and controlled by *him*. Besides, Becky realised, the ice well must be underground, so she would have to dig her way out. She didn't have any tools to do that.

Even though Willow said it wouldn't be possible, maybe there was a clever way to trick the spectre into entering the ice room. If she could get *him* to fall down into the bowl of ice like she just had, that would surely get rid of all *his* energy and destroy *him*. But for the life of her, Becky couldn't think of a way to do that.

Then she remembered an expression she had heard in Religious Studies at school: 'If the mountain will not come to Muhammad, Muhammad must go to the mountain.' She hadn't really understood what it meant at the time, but now it gave her an idea. If she couldn't get the spectre to go into the ice well, could she take a piece of ice out to another part of the house and trick *him* into passing through it? Some of the pieces of ice she had just touched would definitely be big enough to take most, if not all, of *his* energy.

How she was going to lift a piece of the ice out, though, Becky didn't know.

Ice and Fire

Taking hold of the biggest chunk of ice she could feel, Becky planted her feet firmly on the ground and pulled.

It was no good – the ice just slipped through her fingers. She needed something to help her grip with. There was nothing helpful in her bag, so it would have to be a piece of clothing.

Socks – I can use my socks!

Trying not to think of how her feet would feel uncovered in this icy room, she removed her trainers and her thick cotton socks and placed the socks over her hands. She hopped up and down like she was standing on a bed of nails, and quickly put her trainers back on.

Gripping the ice now with sock-covered hands was better, but it didn't make lifting the heavy ice easier. Becky heaved and heaved. It didn't seem like she would get it to move a centimetre, when suddenly the slab jolted up away from the other pieces surrounding it. Becky nearly fell backwards in surprise.

After that, she carefully eased the ice out of the hole. Unsure how long it was, Becky kept pulling for what seemed to be an entire ice age. She hoped that Thatch and the others were managing to distract the spectre on the other side of the metal door and keep *him* away from Finn.

Eventually the ice was free from the well and Becky rested it against a wall. It was a huge slab almost the size of a door!

'The spectre will never survive going through all that!'

She stood to catch her breath, and realised that the cold surrounding her had seeped all the way inside her body, freezing her to the bone. The sooner she got out of the ice well, the better. She gripped one end of the ice slab and pulled it along the tunnel to the door.

Cautiously, she opened the door a tiny way and peered round it. 'Hello? Anyone there?'

'Yes,' replied Willow, floating in the centre of the cellar. 'Rose and I are here. It's safe to come out.'

'What about Finn? Is he OK?'

'I think so. Thatch is fighting the spectre again… They were in the living room last time I checked. *He* hasn't gone near Finn.'

'Don't come too close to me. I'm bringing a big slab of ice through,' Becky warned.

She pushed the door open with her foot and dragged the ice out into the centre of the cellar. Willow and Rose instantly looked pale just from being near to the ice. They moved quickly over to the cellar steps to get away from the cold.

In the faint light Becky was able to see the ice properly for the first time. It was an impressive sight, five centimetres thick at the top and even thicker at the bottom. It seemed to glow and had lots of swirly patterns running through it. Before her hands dropped off, she tried to stand it upright on its thick bottom edge. The ice wobbled ominously for a few seconds, and Becky was worried it might fall and crush her. But then it found its balance and towered above her.

'That is massive. What is the plan now?' asked Willow.

'I somehow need to trick the spectre into going through the ice.'

'If *he* refuses to go in the ice well, *he* won't go through that,' said Rose. 'It just looks like a piece of ice standing up.'

Becky stepped back towards to cellar entrance. Rose was right – the spectre would never fall for it.

'Then I need to disguise the ice in some way – make it look like something the spectre wouldn't be worried about going through.'

She looked around the cellar. There was nothing there to help. She could fetch a sheet from upstairs to put over the ice, or even cover it with straw from the ice well, but why would the spectre be interested in going near either of those things? What she really needed to do was attract him towards the ice.

'Fire!' exclaimed Willow. 'What if you light a fire and put the ice in front of it?'

'But then it would melt too quickly. Although,' Becky's eyes lit up, 'if I light a fire and then angle the ice in the right way, it might reflect the flames and look like a fire itself.'

Willow nodded. 'That's a good idea, Becky. Rose, can you be really brave and keep an eye out at the top of the stairs for the spectre? Just in case *he* comes back before we want *him* to.'

Rose straightened herself determinedly and soared out of the cellar.

Becky took the last couple of bits of wood out of her bag and put them in the fireplace. She opened up her box of matches.

'I've only got one left.'

'One chance to make this work, then. Use it carefully,' said Willow.

Becky bent down and, making sure she shielded the match from the cold, she struck it against the box. A small flame appeared and she pressed the match to the wood until it burned out. The wood seemed to glow red, as if it had caught fire.

But the redness disappeared, replaced by a breath of grey smoke.

Becky closed her eyes – it had failed.

Then she remembered a technique she'd learnt when out camping last year. She breathed in deeply, then blew on the wood. The red glow came back.

She took several more breaths, and blew at the wood powerfully. A small flame popped up on one of the pieces of wood. It got bigger and spread onto the second piece of wood. In no time, the fire was blazing well.

Next, Becky went back to the ice and rotated it slightly, until…

'That's impressive, Becky,' said Willow.

Becky joined Willow by the bottom of the steps. She couldn't see the fireplace from there, but the ice seemed to have disappeared too. The way she had angled it meant that the flames from the fire reflected perfectly onto it. As the orange and yellow colours danced about she had to look very hard to see it was in fact a huge slab of frozen water.

'The spectre will see that and want to take all the heat energy. *He*'ll go straight for it. By the time *he* realises it's ice, it'll be too late.' Becky grinned, feeling confident. 'Do you really think that if *he* passes through that, it will destroy *him*?'

'It's a lot of ice. Even if it doesn't get rid of the spectre completely, it should take away enough of *his* energy that *he* will no longer have control over the house. We would be able to esca—'

A loud roar sounded from somewhere above them, and the house shook slightly. A scream followed – a boy's scream.

'The spectre … has *he* done something to Thatch?' asked Becky.

Rose soared down the steps, tears welling behind her ghostly glasses. Thatch shot in behind her, his face full of fear.

'Thatch! Where's the spectre? What has happened?' asked Willow.

'I'm so sorry. *He* … *he* got away from me. *He*'s up on the third floor. *He*'s got Finn!'

'What?! But Finn's in Willow's room, isn't he?' asked Becky. 'The spectre won't go in there.'

A pained expression formed on Willow's face. 'I broke my promise not to interfere, didn't I? So of course *he*'s going to break *his* promise not to go in my room. How could I be so stupid?'

'I'm sorry,' Thatch said again. 'It's happening, Willow. How it always happens at the end!'

Becky looked from Thatch to Willow. 'What is? What's happening?'

'You need to get to Finn now, Becky,' said Willow. 'Before it's too late.'

Without a second thought, Becky ran up the steps and out of the cellar.

Thatch's Sacrifice

Becky and the ghosts charged through the kitchen.

'There was nothing I could do,' Thatch said. 'None of my usual tactics would get the spectre away from Finn. *He* just ignored me.'

They ran through the hallway and up the stairs. Another thundering roar came, then Finn's scream. It was horrible to listen to.

'*He* wants to get your attention, Becky,' said Willow.

'Well *he*'s certainly got it now!'

'*He*'s trying to trick you,' the ghost-girl continued. 'Be careful.'

But Becky didn't care about being careful. Her friend was in grave danger and it was all her fault. Why did she leave Finn up there? She should have taken him to the ice well.

Up the rope-of-sheets. The spectre's roar deafened her. This time, there was no scream from Finn. Was that a good or a bad thing?

Along the third-floor landing. Into Willow's room.

Becky stopped in her tracks. What she saw then made her feel like she'd breakfasted on nails.

Peter was in the corner of the room, yelling, 'Get off him! Let him go!' and throwing all the parts of the snakes and ladders game at the black mass in front of him. But Peter was barely visible behind the spectre, who was whirling round like a tornado in the middle of the room, blue sparks flying in every direction. And there was Finn, limp and lifeless – *inside the spectre*.

Becky watched with tear-filled eyes as Finn spun round and round in the whirlwind of black, his eyes closed, his skin stretched and pale. The spectre was all too quickly sucking his energy away, consuming Finn whole like a killer snake eating its prey.

'It's … it's too late, isn't it? Finn … he's…'

'You've got to try to do something, Becky,' Willow whispered.

Beside her, Rose couldn't bear to watch and covered her eyes with her plaits. All the ghosts were growing weak from the power of the spectre. They couldn't help if they wanted to.

Becky took several deep breaths. She forced her panic, her fear, into the back of her mind. With a shaky voice she shouted, 'Spectre, let Finn go! I'm here now!'

The spectre didn't seem to be listening. *He* carried on spinning Finn around. Becky remembered back to the spectre's memories – *his* evil laugh. She could almost hear it now. It was sickening; *he* was playing with Finn's body, having fun.

She looked around desperately, trying to find something to distract the spectre. She saw the torch she had left lying by the fireplace and had an idea. She prayed the torch still worked and that the spectre hadn't sucked the energy out of it. Becky picked it up and flicked it on. It sent a beam of light out towards *him*.

'Spectre! It's me you want! Me, Becky, not Finn! Come and get me.'

The spectre stopped spinning round. For a few seconds Finn drifted in the middle of *his* black form. Then Finn collapsed to the floor in a motionless heap. Becky looked to see if he was still breathing but she couldn't tell.

Thatch shot past them all towards his great-nephew, glaring furiously at the spectre.

'Becky, look out!' called Willow.

The spectre was coming at her, at the energy the torch beam was creating. She quickly turned the torch off. The light – the energy *he* wanted to claim – was gone. *He* stopped for a moment, confused.

Becky backed out of the room. 'Willow, please check

that Finn is OK. And, Spectre, if you want to control me, if you want get inside my head, then you'll just have to catch me!'

With that, she ran back along the landing, flicking the torch on and off as the spectre soared after her. Each time the light appeared, the spectre was distracted by it. Then when the light disappeared, it confused *him*. This kept *him* close enough to Becky that she could get *him* to chase her, but far enough away that *he* wasn't able to get inside her mind.

The rope-of-sheets presented a problem, though. Becky couldn't flash the torch while both hands were gripped to the rope, and climbing down it was going to slow her down. She gripped hold of the rope. The torch fell out of her hands and rolled back along the landing. As the spectre approached ever quicker, she just had to abandon it and scramble down the rope-of-sheets.

Becky hadn't even got halfway when the pain in her head increased and memories appeared in front of her...

There was her mum again, the last time Becky had seen her, on the morning before she and Finn set off into the forest. Mum was busy preparing breakfast, while Becky sat and watched. It was Becky's very last memory of Mum...

'Spectre!' a voice called from above.

The memory cleared, and Becky saw Willow whizzing round the spectre. The ghost girl had picked up the torch and was flashing it on and off like Becky had.

It distracted the spectre just long enough for Becky to climb down to the second floor.

'Finn's still breathing,' Willow called after her.

Relieved the worst hadn't happened, Becky continued running. She blocked out the spectre's attempts to get into her head as *he* drew close to her again, and focussed on the cellar. If she could just get to the slab of ice…

By the time she'd reached the kitchen she felt her legs about to give in and she staggered along, tripping over bits of smashed plate strewn across the floor. She got to the top of the cellar steps as the spectre appeared in the kitchen. *He* roared and roared and in one last effort to get to Becky *he* shot forwards and struck her like lightning. Becky was knocked off her feet. She went flying down the steps, bouncing off the hard stone walls until she crashed into the cellar and crumpled onto the floor.

Becky closed her eyes in agony, but she felt the spectre looming over her. She was so close now – the object that would destroy the spectre was waiting just metres away. She saw the bright flames flickering on the ice.

But the spectre was only focussed on one thing – her.

Get up, Becky, get up! her head screamed.

Her body wouldn't respond.

She opened her eyes and through blurred vision saw blue sparks flying as a thin, electric line appeared at the centre of the spectre. *He* was splitting *him*self in half –

just like in the memory she'd seen of Eric. He was about to get into her head, take over her body, control her. And there was nothing she could do!

Becky felt her mouth opening. She tried to close it, but couldn't. As if in slow motion, half the spectre floated towards her head, went through her lips, past her teeth. Her mouth felt like it was burning…

Ahead of her, a light flashed on, like the light at the end of a tunnel that people say you see when you die.

But then the light flashed off. Then on again.

'Oi, Spectre! Look at this.' It was Thatch. He had the torch now.

The burning feeling started to ease. Becky's vision cleared and she saw Thatch there, pulling the spectre away from her. As his hand grabbed the spectre, sparks flew around, seeming to electrocute him. But if Thatch felt any pain he didn't show it. He dragged the spectre out of Becky's mouth, all the time flashing the torch on and off.

Becky blinked several times as she realised what Thatch was doing. He was drawing the spectre away from her and towards the ice.

'Thatch, no! It's not safe for you to do it. You won't survive!'

Thatch turned back to her briefly and smiled. 'Tell Albert I'm sorry.'

'Thatch!'

Becky could only watch as Thatch soared on, both halves of the spectre following him. He saw the ice disguised by fire and ploughed on towards it. The spectre quickly caught up and took hold of Thatch, trying to flip him around. But Thatch carried on forwards. They were locked together now. Thatch grabbed onto the spectre and plunged himself fearlessly into the ice.

The spectre let out an earth-shattering shriek as *he* realised what was about to happen. But there was nothing *he* could do.

As Thatch disappeared into the ice, the spectre went too. A strong burning smell filled the air. *His* dark shape got smaller and smaller as the ice ate *him* up.

Her eyes stinging, Becky didn't look away until every last bit of the spectre was gone. All that remained was the slab of ice, with the reflection of dancing flames flickering over it.

Then, the whole house vibrated violently. It felt like it was about to collapse. A blinding white light came out of the ice. Becky shielded her eyes as it got brighter and brighter and filled the whole cellar.

BANG!

The ice exploded, sending water flying in every direction.

Doorway From Danger

The front door of Thicket House opened. Becky stepped out.

She rubbed happy tears from her eyes. The spectre was gone! They were free!

Becky felt a light forest breeze against her face and the smell of fresh rain filled her nostrils.

The moment the tears had gone, though, Becky started crying again, because of Thatch. He had been so brave, saving her from the spectre and pulling *him* through the ice.

Finn hobbled out behind her and she put a supporting arm around him.

'Are you going to be OK?' she asked.

'I'll be fine,' he said, wincing slightly.

'Do you remember what happened to you?'

Finn thought back. 'Not really. The spectre picked me up, but after that it's all blank.'

'Good,' said Becky.

She turned around to smile at Willow, Rose and Peter, but they weren't there. They had been a minute ago – the ghosts had come down to the front door with the two living children.

Becky looked to Finn. He pointed to the air above them and Becky saw three flashes of colour disappearing. She understood – the ghosts were free now, and they had things they needed to do.

'Do you think Thatch really has gone?' asked Finn.

'I don't know. I think the spectre might have taken Thatch with *him*. Even if he isn't coming back, though, Thatch was a true hero.'

'We'll tell Granddad that. We'll tell him what Thatch did for us and the other ghosts.'

Becky nodded.

The two children started to walk slowly back home through the forest.

***

Becky stepped through the front door of the post office flat and a big rush of relief filled her up.

She heard voices coming from the kitchen.

'We have sent officers out to comb every beach on south Thistlewick, and all the likely places you thought

Becky and Finn could be, but there's been no sign of them, I'm afraid, Mrs Evans.'

'Maybe Albert was right – they could have gone out to sea in a boat together. Or … or maybe they're in the forest!' Mum's voice was filled with panic.

'We will do absolutely everything we can. We have a boat out looking, and I'm going to send my best officers to search the forest.'

At that point Becky stepped into the kitchen. There was Mum, sitting at the table, hunched over a cup of tea. A policewoman from the mainland was sitting beside her and a policeman was standing by the kettle. They all turned around.

Mum clasped a hand to her mouth when she saw her daughter standing there, clothes ripped and muddied, face covered in bruises and scratches.

'Becky!'

'Mum!'

They ran towards each other and Mum wrapped her arms around Becky. The warmth filled Becky's whole body, making up for the two days of cold she had just been through.

***

Becky went straight to bed and slept until late the next morning.

She woke with a start, expecting to be lying on the

cold, hard floorboards of Thicket House. But there in front of her was her own bedroom in the flat above the post office. There was her own wardrobe, her own desk and, surrounding her tightly, her own duvet. Sunlight streamed in through her window.

I'm home! I'm really home!

She heard soothing sounds from along the hallway – Mum humming and preparing breakfast.

Becky got up. She saw her bag lying on the floor and went over. Out of it she pulled Eric's ghost-hunting notebook. She flicked to the page with the title 'Ghosts Seen On Thistlewick'. It was on that page that she had first found Eric's name, which had started her on the adventure into the forest. There it still was, at the bottom of the page.

I never did find Eric's ghost, she thought. *Maybe he's still out there somewhere, floating around the forest.*

Becky took out a pen and added four names to the 'Ghosts Seen On Thistlewick' page: *Peter Shipman, Rose Potts, Thatch Gailsborough and Willow Summercroft.*

She wondered if she would ever see any of them again.

Mum had put together a mammoth breakfast. Stretched across the kitchen table there were endless helpings of cereal, toast, bacon, eggs and sausages.

Over the next hour, Becky told Mum everything, in as much detail as she could manage.

She expected Mum to be really angry, but Mum just looked at her with a mixture of concern and relief.

'Do you believe me, Mum?' Becky asked.

'I can't say I'm sure what to believe. I'm just glad you're home safely now.' Mum rubbed her eyes with a tissue and squeezed Becky's hand. 'I don't think I can stop you being adventurous, can I, Becky Evans? But please promise not to run off again without telling me.'

Becky promised. Then she thought again, remembering how important promises were. She settled on saying, 'At least, I promise I'll try not to.'

Later, Becky set off down Watersplash Lane, making sure she told Mum exactly where she was going. She headed along the coastal path to the harbour. Finn was there, about to go out in a boat with his granddad.

'Want to come fishing?' he called to Becky.

***

'When Thatch disappeared all them years ago, after a few hours I got this feelin' in the pit of my stomach, pulling me into the forest, but I never found him,' Albert explained, his long, silvery beard twitching as he talked.

They were deep out in the crystal blue sea now. Having been trapped in the confines of one house, it was wonderful for Becky to be out in the open again. Finn and Albert had their fishing rods in the water, waiting for a type of fish called a sprat to catch onto their bait.

'I never told no one about Thatch or Thicket House. But I should've. I should've warned Finn about that place. Nobody had a clue where you two had gone. I feared you'd got lost out at sea somehow. That was until yesterday mornin', when I got that same feelin' I'd had with Thatch and I knew you'd gone into the forest. I just knew. I said to them police people that's where you'd be.'

Albert felt a tug on his line, reeled it in and pulled a small, squirming sprat off, dropping it in a bucket. Becky studied him carefully and she could see, even in Albert's old face, that he was Thatch's brother.

'We couldn't have escaped without Thatch, Granddad. He saved us – Thatch was a hero,' said Finn.

The two children told Albert exactly what Thatch had done – that he had saved Finn and Becky from the spectre, and that he wanted Albert to know he was sorry.

'I'm sorry too,' Albert said with a twinkle in his eye, which Becky suspected might be a tear. 'Sorry I let Thatch go in the forest. But I always knew he had it in him to be brave.'

Albert and Finn spent the rest of the afternoon teaching Becky how to fish, and on that day she caught her first ever fish. The sprat wriggled and slipped through her hands as she tried to put it in the bucket. They compared it to the size of the other sprat, and Becky's was the biggest by far.

***

Over the next week two strange stories were told around Thistlewick. One was about the apples that mysteriously appeared on the grave of Stan and Edna Shipman, the parents of a boy who ran away when he was six and never returned. The other story was about Mr Potts's dog, which he had named Rose after his cousin, who had gone missing when he was just a baby. Mr Potts reported that every day that week Rose the dog had already been fed by the time he returned home. The dog had also started playing games with thin air – most unusual behaviour, almost as if she had an invisible friend.

Becky suspected she knew exactly who had been the causes of these stories.

After all this time, though, there had been no sign at all of Willow. Becky longed to see her again, but doubted she ever would.

***

It was the middle of the night and moonlight was pouring into Becky's room when she opened her eyes.

'Hello, Becky.'

At the end of her bed was the silvery image of Willow.

Becky sat up, immediately awake. 'Willow! It's wonderful to see you. How are you?'

'I am well, Becky. More importantly, how are you? Have you got all your memories back now?'

'Yes, they came back as soon as the spectre was gone. I remember who Jimmy is now. It's so good to be home.'

They sat silently, listening to the lapping of the waves out of the window for a minute or two.

'Are Peter and Rose coming?' asked Becky.

'No,' Willow replied simply.

Becky told her about Peter and his parents' grave, and Rose and her cousin's dog.

'They found their families again, all thanks to you, Becky, and Finn and Thatch.'

'Will I see them again?'

'They are gone now.' Reading the puzzled expression on Becky's face, Willow explained, 'We ghosts only exist as long as we have a purpose. Finding their families means Peter and Rose have fulfilled their purpose. By setting them free you made them very happy, Becky.'

'And Thatch? Did the spectre really take Thatch with *him*?'

'I am afraid so. But I do not think Thatch's time was wasted – he served a great purpose. Without him, we would not be here now.'

'What about you, Willow? Have you fulfilled you purpose? Have you found your family?'

'I have searched all over Thistlewick, but with no luck. It seems they moved away from the island many years ago.'

'Oh, Willow, I'm sorry to hear that. Does that mean you don't have a purpose any more?' Becky asked, fearing she was about to lose Willow forever. 'Your purpose could be to be my friend.'

The ghost smiled. 'I do not have a purpose, yet.'

'Yet? Does that mean you will have a purpose soon?'

'Yes,' said Willow. 'I have been talking to other ghosts around Thistlewick, and there are rumours going around that Lord Thistlewick himself will return to the island and something big will happen.'

Becky gasped.

'News has also been spreading of your adventures in recent times,' Willow continued. 'Some ghosts think that you will get involved in Lord Thistlewick's return. They say that if you do, you are going to need my help.'

'Wow! So your purpose is to help me?'

'That will become my purpose,' Willow corrected her. 'For now, I must leave you.'

'But, Willow, when will I see you again?' asked Becky.

'When you next need help, just ask for me. Call my name and I will come. Now, Becky, you should get back to sleep.'

Willow peacefully faded into the distance and Becky lay back on her pillow. Within seconds she was sound asleep, and soon she was dreaming. Dreaming about Lord Thistlewick returning and about the big new adventure Willow had spoken of.

Epilogue

As Becky slept, her mouth slowly opened wide.

A small speck of black escaped from between her lips. It was barely the size of a grain of sand.

The black speck floated up to the corner of Becky's room, just above her wardrobe.

And there, *he* waited.

DOORWAY TO DANGER

is the 2nd book in the 'Ghost Island' series

Becky's adventures continue in book 3:

THE GHOST LORD RETURNS

You can also read about Becky's thrilling first adventure in book 1:

GHOST POST

To find out more, visit:

www.luketemple.co.uk